Sarah was uncomfortable with the idea of eavesdropping on Aunt Charity's and Uncle Ethan's private conversation, but she was anxious to hear what her uncle had to say about Gabrielle.

". . . spends most of her evenings in Christiana Campbell's Tavern listening to the men talk about the Revolution," he was saying as Sarah dropped silently beside Abigail. His words were as clear as though they were still in the room. "We've suspected her for a while, but she's very clever. We haven't been able to catch her passing on what she hears to her British contact, whoever it is. Most likely it's the infamous 'Demon Devon' who eludes our every trap! If only I could get my hands on him!"

"But, Ethan, she's so gracious, so genteel, so . . ."

"So treacherous, Charity," he finished for her. "You heard Sarah say she's interested in me. I'm telling you, she only tutors our children to gain information about my activities and the action of the colonial army. She's a Tory, Charity, a Loyalist of the King of England! She has caused untold damage to our efforts, and she would see me hanged by the British in a heartbeat!"

Sarah gasped, inhaling the horsey scent of boxwood. She turned to find her own shock mirrored in Abigail's wide blue eyes. Her mind whirled dizzily. Surely Uncle Ethan was mistaken! Gabrielle couldn't be a spy!

Be sure to read all the books
in Sarah's Journey

Home on Stoney Creek
Stranger in Williamsburg
Reunion in Kentucky

Also Available as an Audio Book:
Home on Stoney Creek

SARAH'S JOURNEY

STRANGER IN WILLIAMSBURG

Wanda Luttrell

Chariot Books™

*A Division of Cook
Communications Ministries*

Thanks to Sue Reck, my editor, for her help along this journey.

Chariot Books™ is an imprint of Chariot Family Publishing
Cook Communications Ministries, Elgin, Illinois 60120
Cook Communications Ministries, Paris, Ontario
Kingsway Communications, Eastbourne, England

STRANGER IN WILLIAMSBURG
© 1995 by Wanda Luttrell

Cover design by Mary Schluchter
Cover illustration by Bill Farnsworth
Interior illustrations by John Zielinski

First printing, 1995
Printed in the United States of America
99 98 97 96 95   5 4 3 2

Library of Congress Cataloging-in-Publication Data
Luttrell, Wanda.
Stranger in Williamsburg / Wanda Luttrell.
p.   cm.
Summary: Continues the adventures of now twelve-year-old Sarah, who has come from Kentucky to Williamsburg for schooling, only to become embroiled with Revolutionary War spies.
ISBN 0-7814-0902-0
1. United States—History—Revolution, 1775-1783—Juveline fiction. 2. Williamsburg (Va.)—History—Juveline fiction. [1. Spies—Fiction. 2. United States—History—Revolution, 1775-1783—Fiction. 3. Williamsburg (Va.)—History—Fiction. 4. Christian life—Fiction.] I. Title.
PZ7.L97954St   1994
[Fic]—dc20   94-20574
                                                                 CIP
                                                                  AC

Contents

Chapter 1	9
Chapter 2	19
Chapter 3	29
Chapter 4	37
Chapter 5	47
Chapter 6	55
Chapter 7	63
Chapter 8	73
Chapter 9	81
Chapter 10	89
Chapter 11	99
Chapter 12	107
Chapter 13	117
Chapter 14	123
Chapter 15	129
Chapter 16	139
Chapter 17	147
Chapter 18	155
Chapter 19	163
Chapter 20	171
Chapter 21	179
Echoes from the Past	187

For my son,
John Bradley Luttrell,
who makes my journey through life
an adventure.

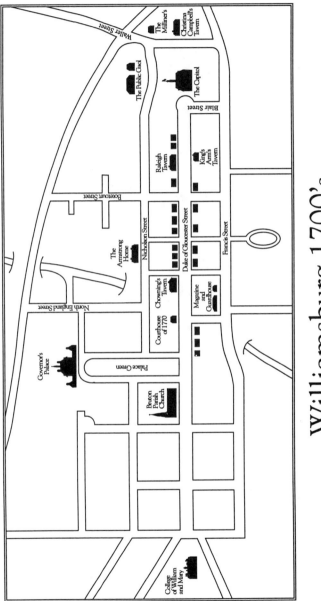

Williamsburg 1700's

There are more people on Duke of Gloucester Street than there were in the whole Kentucky territory! Sarah Moore thought as she stopped at the end of Palace Street where it entered Williamsburg's busy market section. After a month of living here in Virginia's capital city, she still was amazed to see so many people in one place. And, yet, in the midst of the crowd, she felt a pang of loneliness.

Sarah pushed the loneliness aside. She had moped around for over a year in Kentucky, longing for her former home in Virginia. She certainly wasn't going to waste one of the most beautiful June afternoons God had ever made pining to be back in Kentucky, especially when she had been given the rare opportunity to spend it shopping on what had to be the most exciting street in the world!

Behind her, she could hear the shrill piping of flutes and the measured cadence of drums that marked time for the Patriot militia as they drilled on the Palace Green. To her right was the soft pink brick Bruton Parish Church where she went each Sunday to worship with her Aunt Charity's family. To her left, shops and taverns beckoned.

Uncle Ethan had taken them all to the genteel Raleigh Tavern one evening for dinner, and just the memory of the chicken pie made her mouth water.

She hadn't seen Uncle Ethan since that night. He had come home for a brief visit, then had ridden off again on one of his mysterious missions. She had no idea what he did, but she knew it had to do with this war that so concerned everyone in Williamsburg.

Sarah shifted the handle of Aunt Charity's market basket to her other arm. The money her aunt had counted out—the exact amount to pay for the things she wanted from John Greenhow's store—lay in the bottom of the basket, wrapped in a piece of white cloth. Some of the money Pa had sent for Sarah's upkeep while she was living here was wrapped in two pieces of cloth. They were samples of the material she must match with ribbons and buttons for the two new dresses Aunt Charity was making her.

Sarah couldn't help giggling as she remembered the look of horror on her aunt's face when she saw the clothing Sarah had brought with her from Kentucky. It was made of homespun linsey-woolsey and dyed with the juice of berries and hickory bark. Her shoes were deerskin moccasins. Aunt Charity had wasted no time seeing that she was fitted with a couple of hand-me-down dresses and a proper pair of shoes.

Sarah waited for a carriage drawn by a pair of brown horses to pass, then crossed the street to her favorite store in all of Williamsburg. She stood aside to let two gentlemen leave the store, thinking that their black vests over white ruffled shirts, black knee breeches above white stockings, and white powdered wigs tied back with black ribbons gave them the appearance of two strutting crows.

Then she climbed the steps and stood in the open doorway, breathing in the pungent scent of cloves, mingled with the aroma of nutmeg and cinnamon, of scented wax candles and hard round soaps, of fresh-worked wood and leather. She savored the anticipation of plunging into the assortment of merchandise like a longed-for dessert.

Sarah was convinced that just about anything a person could want was there in John Greenhow's store, lined up in cubbyholes along the walls above the tall wooden counters, or in the wooden boxes and bins that crowded the bare wooden floor.

How her ma would love being able to stock up on household supplies in John Greenhow's store, after having to either make do or just do without for over a year in the wilderness! How Pa would glory in being able to buy square iron nails and iron hinges to replace their makeshift wooden pegs and greased leather hinges! How her brother Luke would enjoy the wooden puzzles and the big wooden hoops to roll with a stick down the wide streets of Williamsburg! How little Jamie would love spinning tops and tin whistles!

Again, she was hit by a wave of homesickness for the family she had left in Kentucky. She wished they were here to share the tantalizing taste of the crisp, rolled wafers, or the wonderful little chocolate nonpareils that Nate had bought her that first day in Williamsburg, just before he had left her on Aunt Charity's front stoop.

Nonpareils would always remind her of Nate, she thought, reaching into her pocket to finger the store of coins he had given her so she wouldn't have to ask Aunt Charity every time she wanted some small treat. She said a quick, silent prayer for Nate's safety. Who knew what dangers her oldest brother faced as he fought with the Patriots to win the freedom of the American colonies.

"May I help you, miss?"

Startled, Sarah looked up and located the voice behind the tall counter on her right. The young clerk—surely no older than Luke—was smiling at her, a friendly smile that sent freckles dancing across his face to disappear into the laugh lines around his mouth and at the corners of the bluest eyes she had ever seen.

"I . . . my . . ." She cleared her throat and began again. "I'd like a large cone of brown sugar and an ounce of nutmeg, please," she said, thankful that her voice sounded more assured this time, more grown-up. "Oh, and some raisins," she added hastily, as the boy turned to measure the spice into a twist of brown paper.

He smiled again. "How many raisins?"

Sarah could feel a flush mounting her cheeks. What had Aunt Charity said about the raisins? One scoop? Two scoops?

The clerk held up three different sized scoops and quoted the price of each.

Sarah flushed again. She raised her chin an inch or so. "Two of that size," she said firmly, pointing to one of the scoops, praying the amount would suit Aunt Charity, and that she would have enough money to pay for them.

She must have bought the right portion of raisins, though, for Aunt Charity had sent exactly the amount of money the clerk named. Quickly, she counted the coins into his hand, thanked him, and moved away to the back of the store, tucking her purchases into the basket on her arm. When she looked back, he was waiting on another customer. Sarah turned, with relief, to attempting to match the squares of fabric Aunt Charity had sent, but there just wasn't any ribbon that would do. The buttons in the small wooden bins weren't to her liking, either.

The pleasant-faced woman behind the counter must have noticed her frustration. "There'll be more arriving any day now on Mr. Greenhow's next boat down the James," she offered.

Sarah chewed her lower lip. She looked down at Abigail's drab, brown hand-me-down dress. Now that Aunt Charity had agreed that it was time for some new clothes of her own, she didn't want to wait for the next boat to come down the river before her new blue Sunday dress and the nice, gray everyday frock could be finished.

"If you're in a hurry, you might try the milliner's down the street, across from the magazine," the clerk suggested helpfully.

Sarah knew the magazine was that funny little eight-sided brick building where the Patriot soldiers stored their guns and ammunition. She was almost there when her attention was drawn across the street to where a young girl stood behind a small table in front of Chowning's Tavern, drawing a golden liquid from a wooden keg into customers' cups.

All at once, Sarah realized her mouth was as dry as if it were full of sawdust. A cold cup of sweet apple juice made from fresh June apples would taste wonderful, she thought, fingering Nate's coins.

Aunt Charity would have a fit, though, if she went anywhere near Chowning's. She said it was a "low-class, bawdy place, not fit for decent ladies to pass by, much less visit!" Sarah's cousin Tabitha had whispered that there was gaming and riotous behavior among the tavern's evening patrons who gathered there to eat, drink grog and other liquors, and gamble. If so, it was nothing like the Raleigh!

Nevertheless, Tabitha and Abigail had been by Chowning's many times, for Tabitha had her eye on a certain young man who served tables and cleaned up after the tavern's midday and evening meals. Unwilling to go alone, she begged and bribed her younger sister to accompany her at precisely 2:15 on many afternoons, to catch a glimpse of Seth Coler as he came out to dump slop in the pigs' trough behind the tavern.

In fact, it was this very habit that had led to Sarah's opportunity to visit the shops alone today. Aunt Charity had caught Tabitha and Abigail standing in the alley outside Chowning's just last week. She had confined the girls to the house and yard for a week. And, busy with preparations for the week's baking, Aunt Charity had bestowed on Sarah the unheard-of privilege of doing her shopping.

Now Sarah stood at the edge of the dusty street, with her mouth growing drier and drier. She could almost taste the apple juice, smooth and sweet as honey on her tongue. She could feel Nate's coins practically burning a hole in her pocket. And, almost before she realized what she was doing, she was standing in front of the girl, holding out her money.

The girl smiled at her from under a white mobcap that did its best to hide thick, tangled brown curls. The smile displayed a missing tooth, but it lit up her brown eyes. "You have no cup? I can sell you this tin mug for . . ." The girl

frowned in concentration as she counted out the necessary coins from Sarah's hand.

Absently, Sarah watched the girl drop the coins into the pocket of her blue and white striped skirt, straighten her white apron over it, and tuck in her full white blouse. Sarah hadn't meant to spend so much on one cup of juice, but the mug was charming. It held an etching of a tall cedar tree holding some large bird with its wings outspread, ready to fly. From now on, she could carry the little cup with her, and next time, she would only have to pay for the drink. Sarah turned to look for a bench to sit down and enjoy her cold, sweet juice.

Suddenly, there beside the courthouse, Sarah saw a sight she had not seen in the whole month she had spent in the colonial capital. The wooden stocks (which reminded her of a yoke for harnessing oxen) held a man, bent over, with his arms and neck locked into the holes. His dark forehead, under a mass of tight, white curls, glistened with sweat, and she saw him run his tongue over cracked lips.

As she stared in horror, he raised his head and looked directly into her eyes. Then, at the demand of the cruel stocks, he dropped his head again, but not before Sarah had seen the look of resigned misery in his dark eyes.

She wanted to turn away, to go on about her business down the street. But that one glimpse of the man's eyes held her rooted to the spot. All at once, Sarah knew what she had to do. Carefully holding her cup, she walked the few steps that separated her from the stocks.

"Sir," she began hesitantly. There was no response, and she cleared her throat and tried again. "Sir, would you like a cup of apple juice?" She extended the one she had just bought toward him.

At last, the man looked up. Amazement crossed his face as he took in her earnest look and extended hand offering the cup. "You talkin' to me, missy?" His voice was as cracked as his parched lips.

She nodded. "Would you like this cup of cold apple juice?"

The old man rolled his eyes to see who was watching. "Are you sure?" he whispered. Then thirst overcame his amazement at the offer. "Missy, if you'll just put the cup to my lips, I'd be much obliged. I can't . . . ."

Sarah realized that the stocks would not allow him to reach for the cup or move it to his lips. She held the cup, and the man drank from it thirstily. She held it again, and he finished it.

"The Lord bless you for your kindness, missy," he murmured.

"My name is Sarah," she said, placing the empty cup in her basket, feeling more refreshed than if she had swallowed the juice herself. "Why are you in the stocks?" she asked. She knew that the punishment was usually reserved for thieves and other lawbreakers.

"Some of the townspeople think ole Marcus is uppity, with the manners and skills he learned working at the palace. They don't think the governor's lady should have given him free papers when she left. But they put me in the stocks because they think I'm a Tory!" He spat on the ground in disgust.

Sarah hadn't the faintest idea what the old man meant, except she knew that a Tory was someone who remained loyal to King George and England, instead of supporting the Patriots in their quest for freedom.

"Go on, Miss Sarah," he said gently, "before you get in trouble for talking to me. My time in the stocks will be over at sundown, or sooner if Governor Henry comes back from Richmond and finds out where I am. I can make it now. The Lord bless you!" he repeated.

Reluctantly, Sarah backed away and walked slowly on down the street toward the milliner's, haunted by the image of the misery in the sad, dark eyes of the man in the stocks.

2

Absently, Sarah climbed the front steps to the open door of the milliner's and went inside. She held out her samples of material and requested the ribbons and buttons her aunt wanted, barely noticing the merchandise that lined the walls and counters of the small shop, or the middle-aged woman who came to wait on her.

When the milliner's clerk came back to say she couldn't match her material, at least not until a new shipment came on the next boat down the James, Sarah was almost out the front door before she thought to ask if there was another milliner in town.

The clerk frowned, then grudgingly answered that there was a new shop down on Waller Street behind the Capitol, next to Christiana Campbell's Tavern.

Another tavern? Sarah thought. Which would displease Aunt Charity more—to go home without the buttons and trimming she wanted, or to go near another tavern? Sarah had already broken the rules once today by buying apple juice in front of Chowning's. What kind of place was Christiania Campbell's Tavern? Would Aunt Charity consider it "bawdy" too?

Her aunt certainly knew what she wanted, though, and when she wanted it. Sarah sighed. It might be better to risk Aunt Charity's disapproval of her walking near another tavern, than to incur her wrath over an uncompleted errand. Besides, she did want those new dresses!

Sarah walked down Duke of Gloucester Street to where it ended. She turned right onto short little Blair Street, which led right past the Capitol. She always felt a thrill of excitement when she thought of the House of Burgesses meeting there to make Virginia's laws. Kentucky's laws, too, for that matter, since Kentucky territory belonged to Virginia.

The Capitol was built like a soft red brick castle. It had two round wings which were joined by a long, straight section that was topped by a cupola. Nathan had told her that not long ago, the British flag flew from the cupola, and Williamsburg was the capital of the British colony of Virginia. He said that the British governor disbanded the House of Burgesses because they protested against unfair laws England imposed upon the colonies. Then, at the start of the Revolution, the governor had taken his household back to England, and now the new flag of the American states waved in the breeze above the Capitol.

Sarah remembered a friend of her pa's, back in Kentucky, saying, "I ain't never gonna bow my knee to no British king!" Well, it seemed that almost everybody in Williamsburg felt the same way. Of course, there were a few Tory families around who still pledged loyalty to England

and King George. But, for the most part, every able-bodied man in and around the town had declared himself ready to put his life on the line for freedom.

She stopped in front of the Capitol, chewing her lip. Where on earth was Waller Street? She knew it joined Nicholson one block over from Duke of Gloucester. Aunt Charity's house was on Nicholson. But she had thought Duke of Gloucester went all the way down past the Capitol.

Not wanting to waste time retracing her steps back to more familiar territory, Sarah decided to take the chance that the street ahead would join Waller a block over. She turned left at the end of Blair onto Francis, and was relieved to see that just ahead it did join Waller, again to the left.

There on her right was Christiana Campbell's sprawling white tavern. And just beyond it was a neat little brown cottage with a swinging sign that read "Milliner."

In keeping with what she thought would be Aunt Charity's wishes, Sarah walked past the tavern on the other side of the street. Then she crossed Waller and headed up the brick path that led from the wooden front gate to the milliner's shop.

At the front stoop, she stopped to reach into her basket to make sure she had the money and Aunt Charity's samples. Then she pushed against the door and heard the jingling of brass bells announce her entry. Sarah stood waiting for her eyes to adjust from the bright sunlight outside to the dim interior of the shop.

"May I help you, *chérie?*" a soft, husky voice inquired.

Behind a tall counter at the back of the room, Sarah saw the most gorgeous creature she ever had seen. The woman

smiled at her from soft pink lips and amused dark eyes. Her arched red-gold eyebrows perfectly matched the thick coils of dark copper hair piled high on her regal head.

"I won't bite, *chérie*," the woman laughed. "You wanted some goods from the milliner, *oui?*"

"I . . . I . . . Yes, ma'am," Sarah finally managed to stammer. She tore her gaze from the pink nails of the small, dainty hands resting on the counter, to the high, cream-colored lace collar that seemed to hold up the slender neck.

For a moment, Sarah couldn't for the life of her, think why she had come here. The woman was like something from a storybook—a princess, a queen, an angel.

She fumbled in Aunt Charity's basket, and came up with the samples of material to match with the ribbons and buttons. She recited her needs and handed the woman the scraps of material.

★ Chapter Two ★

"Ah, yes, I am sure that I have the perfect match for these, *chérie*. Wait here, *s'il vous plaît?*" She swept down the aisle with a rustle of silk and a whiff of some sweet, musky perfume. Sarah leaned dizzily against the counter.

"By the way, I am Gabrielle Gordon, the milliner," the woman introduced herself, placing samples of ribbon and buttons on the material for Sarah to see. She seemed to be waiting for an answer. "And you, *chérie?*" she prompted.

Finally, Sarah came to herself enough to stammer, "I am Charity Armstrong's niece, Sarah Moore. From Kentucky," she added.

"Kentucky!" the milliner exclaimed, turning to study Sarah intently. "It is a province of Virginia, is it not? A place of wildness and savages, I am told. So how do you come to be so well-mannered? Such an elegant young lady?"

Sarah turned a deeper rose than the milliner's dress. "Well . . . I . . . my . . . we . . ." She wanted to cry. This beautiful creature would think she was one of the very savages she mentioned. Why was her tongue so tied today?

"Never mind, *chérie*. Gabrielle must learn to control the teasing. I am afraid I have embarrassed you. Please forgive me. Do you know why I am called a milliner?" Sarah knew she was trying to give her time to collect her thoughts, and simply shook her head no.

"Originally, the word was 'milaner,' one who comes from or imports goods from Milan, Italy. But what do Italians know about fashion, *chérie?*" She laughed a short, husky laugh that sent shivers of delight down Sarah's spine. "I, Mademoiselle Sarah, import my goods from Paris, France, which sets the fashion for the world!"

Sarah knew no more about fashion than the milliner's scorned Italians, but she found that she could laugh with her this time. She listened raptly to the soft voice, with its attractive French accent and a foreign word or two thrown in now and then, as the milliner told her about the hats and muffs, the fans and gloves, the jewelry, purses, shoes, and ribbons that lay on shelves behind and below the tall counters that filled three sides of the small room.

Finally, she wrapped Sarah's purchases in a piece of brown paper and tied it neatly with string. She snipped the string with embroidery scissors, and exchanged the package for the money Aunt Charity had supplied from Pa's purse. As she counted Sarah's change into her hand, the milliner said, "Charity Armstrong's niece, you say?"

Sarah nodded.

"Then you are also the niece of Ethan Armstrong, are you not?"

"Uncle Ethan is married to my Aunt Charity," Sarah explained, "my mother's sister."

"I suppose you have not seen the uncle much since you came? He seems to always be away on this business of his, whatever it is." Gabrielle looked at her questioningly from the corner of her eye.

"No," Sarah agreed, "he is not at home often. He is always off on some errand. I have no idea where he goes or what he does."

"Ah, *oui*," the milliner commented with a knowing smile. "There are people who share your curiosity! Perhaps, someday. . . . But tell me, Mademoiselle Sarah, why have you left the wild Kentucky to come live with your aunt and uncle here in Williamsburg?"

"I was born in Miller's Forks, Virginia, but my family moved to Kentucky a little over a year ago. My brother came for me last month to bring me back to Virginia to study."

"And what do you study, Mademoiselle Sarah? The social graces? The music and dancing? Or do they do such things in the wild Kentucky?"

Sarah knew the milliner was teasing her again, but she answered seriously, "We need a school on Stoney Creek, where my family and some others live. I plan to be a teacher," she added proudly.

"Ah, the *institutrice!*" Gabrielle exclaimed. "But, *chérie,* I myself am the teacher! The tutor, as they say here. Of course, the teachers in the schools here all are the gentlemen, and only the boys are allowed to attend. I teach the young ladies to speak and write and serve tea properly, to embroider, to play the harpsichord and dance. All the social graces. But the daughters and niece of Ethan and Charity Armstrong already have a tutor, *oui?*"

Sarah shook her head. "No, ma'am. My cousins had a tutor until the royal governor's household fled back to England. The tutor went with them, and Tabitha and Abigail haven't had a tutor since."

"July, 1775," Gabrielle sighed. "I remember it well. Governor Dunmore and his household crept out of Williamsburg before dawn, like the mice afraid of the cat. And with them was the governess who tutored several young ladies from families around the town, along with the governor's own household.

"I met them in Boston, as they waited for a ship to take them back to England," she continued. "They strongly urged me to go with them, but I had my heart set on a milliner's shop, and eventually made my way here to Williamsburg. Three weeks ago, I opened this shop." She sighed. "Sometimes I wish I had gone with them, *chérie.*"

Sarah gasped. "Are you a Tory then?" she choked out,

"a supporter of the King?" She couldn't stand here passing the time of day with a Tory with both Nate and Uncle Ethan being such Patriots!

The milliner spread her hands and shrugged her shoulders. "The blood of Gabrielle Gordon wars in her veins, *chérie*. My father's cool English blood demands loyalty to the King of England, while my mother's hot French blood cheers for the feisty colonists France is silently supporting in this Revolution." She smiled at Sarah. "And I suppose you are a hot-blooded Patriot, also, Mademoiselle Sarah?" she asked, "like your Uncle Ethan?"

Sarah smiled back at her, in spite of her misgivings about Tories. "I have a brother up north somewhere fighting for the Patriots. He wouldn't like me associating with Tories, I am sure," she said honestly.

"Ah, well, you can be friends with the French Gabrielle and forget the English Gordon, can you not, *chérie?* After all, most of these fiery Patriots once swore allegiance to the British crown, did they not?"

"Yes, Miss Gordon," Sarah answered politely.

"*Non, non, chérie!* You must call me by the French Gabrielle."

"Yes, ma'am," Sarah answered. Then seeing the pout on the milliner's rosy lips, corrected hastily, "Yes, Gabrielle. Ma'am."

Gabrielle smiled. "That's better, *chérie*. And tell your Aunt Charity that Gabrielle—the best tutor in all of Williamsburg—is available to tutor her daughters and her niece, if she so desires. Of course, if she wishes you to be tutored during the day, you would have to come here, since I must see to my shop. Or I could come to you in the evenings, if she prefers."

★ Chapter Two ★

"Yes, m . . . ah, Gabrielle," Sarah stammered, backing out of the shop and almost falling backward off the stoop. She felt the flush mounting her cheeks again. Gabrielle surely thought her the most awkward girl in both the colonies and the Kentucky territory! Still, she couldn't resist one last look back.

As though she hadn't noticed Sarah's clumsiness, the milliner gave a little wave with one hand. Sarah waved back. Then she turned and ran all the way up Waller Street to where it joined Nicholson. She was very late, and Aunt Charity would be counting the minutes as carefully as she would every cent of the change Sarah could hear jingling in her basket as she ran.

3

Sarah stopped outside her aunt's front gate to catch her breath. Then she opened the gate and headed up the brick sidewalk, letting the iron ball and chain swing the gate shut behind her.

The door of the neat brick house opened suddenly, and Hester Starkey scowled down at her. "Where've you been?" she asked. "Your aunt will be asking questions, and you'd better have answers!"

Sarah looked up at the dour old housekeeper. Her hair was pulled back so tightly into a tuck that it stretched the skin over her cheekbones. Sarah felt sure the unfriendly face had been set in those hard lines for so many years that it would crack like old china if she tried to smile. Probably the woman had never smiled in her entire life.

It didn't pay to be on Hester's bad side, though, so Sarah simply answered, "Yes, ma'am," as she edged past her and entered the dim front hall.

"Sarah, is that you?"

Sarah swallowed hard and cleared her throat. "Yes, Aunt Charity, and I've got some wonderful news!"

Her aunt appeared in the parlor doorway. "Have you now?" she asked doubtfully, eying her niece from eyes that could have been those of her sister, Della, Sarah's mother. Only Aunt Charity's lacked the warmth and love Sarah was accustomed to seeing in her mother's eyes. *Aunt Charity's hair is lighter than Ma's, too,* she thought, *and it has that red-gold tint, but it would be just as curly, if she ever let it down.*

"Yes, ma'am," Sarah went on, summoning all the excitement she could muster into her voice. "I've found a tutor for Tabitha, Abigail, and me!"

"A tutor?" her aunt repeated. "I presume you know I require a lady, and one with sundry accomplishments to bring to the job?"

"Yes, ma'am," Sarah repeated.

"Well, speak up, child! Who is this tutor you've found? Where does she live? I know everybody in Williamsburg, and I know of no tutor since the governor's family left."

"Her name is Gabrielle Gordon. She lives on Waller Street, and she's a milliner. I had to go there to get . . ."

"I know of no millinery shop on Waller Street," Aunt Charity interrupted. She ticked off the street's buildings and their owners on her fingers. "Then there's Christiana Campbell's Tavern, and next to that, the small brown house rented by the apothecary's apprentice. To my knowledge," she finished, "that's the entire street."

"Gabrielle Gordon's house is that little brown one next to Christiana Campbell's," Sarah said. "I suppose the apprentice moved out. She hasn't been there long. Anyway, her shop is in the front room, and she lives in the back. She said she could teach us there during the day, or here in the evenings."

Aunt Charity smoothed her hair, then her spotless white apron. "All right, Sarah. I'll talk with this Miss Gordon and see if she's suitable. Did you get the things I ordered?"

Sarah handed her the basket. "Your order came to exactly the amount you sent, and the change from Pa's money is in the bottom, wrapped the way you sent it." Sarah was proud of her success with the shopping, and hoped it would please her aunt so she would be allowed to do it again sometime.

As Aunt Charity counted the change and inspected her purchases, Sarah stuck her hand in her pocket to finger the few coins she had left. She was surprised to discover the forgotten tin cup. Quickly, she covered its bulge with her hand so her aunt would not see it.

"Very good, Sarah," Aunt Charity said, with a tight little smile of approval. "You may go to your room and freshen up before supper. Tabitha and Abigail are helping Hester prepare the table this evening."

Sarah breathed a sigh of relief as she forced herself to walk sedately down the long hall and up the stairs to the bedroom she shared with Abigail. She was sorry her cousins were still being punished by having to do kitchen duty, but she was glad to have a few moments to herself. She was glad, too, that Aunt Charity had been distracted by her news of a tutor, and had not asked too many questions.

Sarah hoped her aunt would approve of Gabrielle Gordon. She tingled with excitement just thinking of spending time with the beautiful half-French, half-English lady. And she hoped they would go to the milliner's cozy little brown house to study, away from the cold, appraising eyes of the Armstrong household.

Aunt Charity wasn't really unkind, she reminded herself. She was just a serious woman, busy with her household affairs, especially since Uncle Ethan was away so much.

Again, Sarah wondered briefly where he went and what he did on those long journeys that sent him back home exhausted, but in a hurry to leave again. She wished he were there more often, for the place was livelier and more pleasant when her uncle was home.

Fifteen-year-old Tabitha was wrapped up in plans for her marriage in a year or so to Seth Coler, though he didn't know it yet! Tabby thought of nothing but learning to run a home, making things for her dowry chest, and getting down to Chowning's before her unsuspecting chosen one came out to slop the pigs.

Sarah entered the big room with dark, heavy furniture that she shared with thirteen-year-old Abigail. Abigail was half a year older than Sarah and never missed a chance to point that out. She also never missed a chance to point out the fact that the room they shared belonged to her. She was always telling Sarah to use only this little space in the closet and that tiny drawer in the dresser, and to sit on this chair and not that one, and to make sure she slept on her own edge of the tall, four-poster bed, and that she didn't touch anything at all of Abigail's.

Sarah wished she could share a room with seven-year-old Megan, instead. Only Megan made her feel welcome in this house. Meggie's small, cozy room was at the back of the house, tucked under the sloping eaves, and Megan left no doubts about her wishes to share everything with Sarah. She wanted to be with her every minute.

★ Chapter Three ★

Sarah poured a little water from the tall, pink-flowered pitcher into the basin and washed her face and hands. She dried them carefully on the linen towel and hung it back on the rail at the side of the washstand, exactly as she had found it.

She peered into the small oval mirror, and inspected her face hopefully. She sighed. It seemed that all the beauty in the family had been unfairly distributed among her aunt's children. Tabitha, with her soft brown hair and contented gray eyes, looked more like Sarah's ma than she did. And Abigail had the fragile, china-doll look of Aunt Charity, with pale blue eyes and blonde hair with a hint of red in it. Even little Megan promised to be a beauty someday, with her father's laughing brown eyes and dark hair, and with the added blessing of Aunt Charity's curls.

"And here you stand, Sarah Moore, in all your glory!" she mocked. "That hair as straight as a stick, and those green cat's eyes, and freckles scattered over the Irish nose between them!" She sighed again and smoothed the skirts of Abigail's outgrown dress, rediscovering the cup hidden in her pocket.

Where could she put it for safekeeping? In Miller's Forks, she had had a room of her own in which to keep her treasures. In Kentucky, she had had a small wooden box she kept under her bed. Here, there really wasn't much room in her one tiny drawer, though she had few possessions to store there, anyway.

Could she set the cup on the shelf above her end of the closet? No, Abigail had things in there. She would find the cup and Sarah would have to explain. Somehow, she didn't want to share her cup, or its story, with Abigail, or with anyone.

She examined the etching on its side. The cedar tree reminded her of the one in the Armstrongs' backyard, out behind Meggie's bedroom window. That tree seemed almost human sometimes. When the wind blew gently, it murmured and whispered to itself. When the wind blew hard, it moaned and sighed in agony. She often sat listening to it, trying to figure out what secrets it might be trying to tell her.

The tree on the cup looked like a cedar, with its branches set in motion by the wind. And that bird clinging to its top branch—was it an eagle? The Patriots sometimes used an eagle to represent their cause. Did this sketch have something to do with the war? She had no idea what the design meant, if anything, but the cup would always be special to her, for she had bought it with Nate's money; she had shared its contents with someone in need; and on the day she had bought it, she had met Gabrielle.

Finally, Sarah tucked the cup into the small deerskin traveling bag Ma had made her for the trip back to Virginia. Surely Abigail wouldn't look in there. She certainly had no business doing so!

Sarah had just replaced the bag in the closet and shut the door when she heard Megan calling her.

"There you are, Sarah!" the little girl exclaimed, bounding into the room. She flew across the floor, and caught Sarah around the waist in a hug as big as her small arms could manage.

"It's time for supper, Sarah," Megan announced, tugging at her hand and heading for the door. "Old sourpuss Hester has fixed fried chicken, and no matter how mean she is, her fried chicken is 'licious!"

"Megan!" Sarah scolded. "You mustn't call Mrs. Starkey

'sourpuss'! Even if Abigail does."

"Well, she is a sourpuss, Sarah. I know that if she ever smiled her face would just break all over."

Sarah smothered a giggle, recalling her own thoughts about Mrs. Starkey and cracked china, as she ran down the stairs behind Megan.

The little girl threw her one last crooked grin before they entered the dining room to take their places at the side of the long, dark table covered with a snow-white cloth and steaming dishes of food.

As usual, Sarah felt a lump gather in her throat at the sight of her ma's blue-flowered china sitting there on somebody else's table. It had belonged to Sarah's grandmother—Ma and Aunt Charity's mother—and Ma had loved it dearly. It always held a place of honor in her corner cupboard in Miller's Forks, but Ma had given the china to Aunt Charity when they left for Kentucky, afraid it would get broken on the long hard journey through the wilderness. She had taken only the teapot which already had a chip in its spout.

Sarah swallowed the lump in her throat, and bowed her head as Aunt Charity offered thanks to God for the food. She would not think about where the pretty flowered china had come from, she vowed, as she passed her plate for a helping of crisp fried chicken, and biscuits covered with thick, white milk gravy. She caught Megan's wink, as the little girl sank her teeth into a crunchy drumstick.

By the time she had finished that first plateful, plus a helping of peas, spiced apples, and potatoes dripping with creamy, fresh-churned butter, Sarah was too full to care that Aunt Charity never served dessert except on Sundays and when Uncle Ethan was home.

"It's your turn to dry!" Abigail hissed loudly in Sarah's ear when they had finished the meal. But Aunt Charity heard the comment.

"You may help clear the table, Sarah, and then you are free until bedtime," she said firmly, staring hard at Abigail. "Tabitha and Abigail will do the dishes again tonight."

Sarah stood up and began gathering plates. Hester Starkey usually did the dishes, with some help from the girls with clearing the table. Obviously, Tabitha and Abigail's punishment had not ended.

Sarah carried the dishes to the wooden sink in the kitchen, where Mrs. Starkey already had a tub of steaming water waiting. Then she went back into the dining room.

"May I go for a walk, Aunt Charity?" she asked.

Her aunt studied her intently for several seconds. "Yes, Sarah," she agreed finally. "You may go anywhere along Nicholson Street or one block north, but be back before dark."

"Yes, ma'am, I will," Sarah promised. Duke of Gloucester was one block south, but she had already visited Duke of Gloucester today.

"Williamsburg gardens are beautiful this time of year, Sarah," Aunt Charity called after her.

"Yes, ma'am!" Sarah called as she slipped out the back door, eager to get away from the house before she was discovered by Megan.

Normally, she would have been glad of the little girl's company, and she felt a twinge of guilt for leaving her behind. But she had a very special destination in mind this evening, and she wanted to go there alone.

It is so beautiful here by the canal! Sarah thought, watching two graceful white swans glide over the quiet water below the grassy bank where she sat. Here, the water was so close she could have dabbled her feet in it, but on either side of her, the banks grew steeply toward small wooden bridges that joined the sides of the canal.

She sighed, wishing she could stay in the peaceful gardens forever. The war, which was constantly on everyone's mind and tongue in Williamsburg, seemed as remote as it had back in Kentucky, like a story of once-upon-a-time told around a winter fire. It touched neither the beautiful flowers and trees, nor the swans and the geese.

The swans reminded her of Gabrielle, with their long, graceful necks and royal bearing. Then Sarah laughed. She spotted an old goose that reminded her of Aunt Charity, ordering her goslings into the water with no

nonsense accepted. Then she sailed off downstream, with all of them following obediently in a row. *Like my cousins and me!* Sarah thought. *Well, most of the time,* she amended honestly.

Footsteps on the graveled path reminded her that she did not have permission to be here, and her heart skipped a beat. Megan had warned her not to go into the gardens, but surely no one would mind. She had no intention of harming anything in this lovely spot.

Sarah threw a quick glance over her shoulder, but saw no one. Still, she would feel better if she weren't caught, so she slipped up the bank and through the trimmed yews and boxwoods that the gardener's shears had shaped into green, growing sculptures. From there, she crossed a small plot of grass and entered the orchard. She had never been this far into the gardens.

Sarah listened. The footsteps seemed to be closer now. Desperately, she looked around for a better hiding place, and her gaze fell on a thick row of clipped green holly bushes. She ducked through a doorway formed by the gardener's shears and a small wooden gate, and found herself on a narrow, grassy path between thick, tall greenery that overlapped above her head like a leafy cave.

It's smothery in here! she thought, drawing in a deep breath heavy with the musky scent of growing things. But outside her hiding place, she could still hear the crunch of gravel under shoes. Was her pursuer in the orchard now? She eased quietly down the path to where it turned sharply right. She followed the turn, then another and another, finding herself deep in the green tunnel.

She had spent weeks traveling through dense wilderness on her journey to Kentucky and on the one back to Virginia, but never had she felt so oppressed by moist, heavy air as she did here on this twisting path among the thick, scratchy bushes. She turned to retrace her steps to the entrance, but every time she thought she had discovered the way, she found herself hopelessly trapped in yet another green, box-like room, or on a dead-end path.

Sarah tried desperately to fill her lungs with air, but she couldn't get enough. She could feel panic rising. She had to get out of there! Frantically, she pushed against the prickly branches, but they grew so thickly she could not force her way through.

Suddenly, she could stand it no longer, and began to sob aloud.

"Ho! You there in the maze! What are you doing in there?" a man's voice called.

All at once, her need for rescue outweighed her fear of

discovery. "I'm trying to get out!" she cried. "Help me!" Her voice caught on a sob.

"Work your way toward the sound of my voice," the man said.

She ran down one path, only to come to another dead end. She ran back and took a second path. She was totally confused. Where was he? "I can't . . ." She gasped for air. "I can't! . . ."

"Over here, missy. Come along, now. You can do it," the voice soothed. "Come right toward my voice. You're doin' fine." He kept up a running, one-sided conversation to guide her, as she followed path after path until, finally, she took a last turn and saw a tall, dark shadow imposed across the sunlight at the opening.

What would become of her now that she had been caught trespassing? Would she be arrested and carried off to gaol? Would she be put in the stocks in front of the courthouse where people would mock her as they passed?

The smothery tangle of bushes seemed safe and comforting now, and as she watched the man come toward her, she wished she had stayed there. She moved back a step.

"Miss Sarah, is that you?" the man asked, removing his hat respectfully. Tight, white curls sprang up as their restraint was removed, and she saw that it was the man she had given her apple juice as he stood in the stocks. What was his name? Moses? Martin?

"Well, missy, it's a blessin' ole Marcus came along when he did, or you might have had to spend the night in that maze!"

Sarah inhaled, gratefully drawing fresh air into her lungs.

★ Chapter Four ★

"I caught a glimpse of you on the bank of the canal when I came down to throw some stale bread crumbs to the swans and geese," he said, "but you disappeared into the orchard before I could recognize you."

"What are you going to do with me?" she managed to whisper. She knew she was guilty of trespassing. There was no use trying to deny it. She had been caught in the act.

Marcus threw back his head and laughed a deep, long laugh. "Mercy me, Miss Sarah!" he said. "Ain't you the same young lady who gave me a drink of cold apple juice on a hot summer's day, when I was in no position to get one for myself?"

She nodded her head, wondering what that had to do with her present predicament.

"And don't you think ole Marcus appreciates that kindness?"

She didn't know what to say. Was he not going to? . . .

"Besides," he went on, "these grounds belong to the Commonwealth of Virginia now. Why, Virginia's governor, Patrick Henry himself, now lives in this palace that was built for the king's governor. And, so long as you keep out of the ballroom gardens where Governor Henry takes his morning and evening walks, you won't be in his way at all."

"I know I had no business coming here, sir, without permission," she stammered. "I'm sorry."

He waved her apology away. "You just enjoy these gardens, Miss Sarah. Ole Marcus works hard to keep them looking good, and he's happy to share them with the likes of you. Things just seem more special when you can share them. And I'll tell the governor all about it, so you won't need to fear being caught again."

Sarah felt tears gathering behind her eyes at his

kindness. And all because she had impulsively given him her cup of apple juice earlier today! It was like that verse in the Bible that said, "Cast thy bread upon the waters, and after many days, it will return to you."

"Thank you, sir," she said, with a curtsy.

"You just call me Marcus, Miss Sarah. And if ever you need a friend, all you have to do is yell, and ole Marcus will come runnin'!"

"Thank you, Marcus," she said again.

He placed the old hat back on his head and turned to go. Then he turned back. "It seems to me that I've seen you somewhere before, besides in front of the stocks on Duke of Gloucester Street."

Sarah was sure she'd never seen him anywhere else. "I'm Charity and Ethan Armstrong's niece from Kentucky," she explained.

"Kentucky?" he repeated, and Sarah saw pain shadow his eyes.

"Do you know someone in Kentucky?" she asked, wondering if he had family there who had died or been killed. He looked so sad.

He shook his head, walking toward the ballroom gardens. "I don't know, missy," he said. "My wife and child were sold to a slave trader who claimed he was heading for Kentucky. But I never believed it. From what I hear, the market for slaves in Kentucky is small. I think he took them farther south to be sold to some cotton planter."

"Sold?" she echoed in horror, skipping a step to catch up with him. "But you said the governor's lady gave you free papers before she went back to England. Didn't she free your family too?"

"Dulcie and Sam didn't belong to Governor Dunmore.

42

They belonged to a James River plantation owner who would have sold his own mother for two farthings!" He stopped walking and stared sadly off toward the palace, his thoughts obviously much farther south than the elegant pink brick building in front of them. "I've just always hoped they were bought by a kinder master," he added.

"Did you ever try to find them, Marcus?" Sarah asked.

He nodded. "I finally picked up the trail of that trader in South Carolina, at the slave market in Charleston. But, out of all the poor folks sold on that block, nobody could remember a beautiful, brown-skinned woman with a little boy who looked just like his pa clinging to her hand. To them, you know, we all look alike."

Sarah didn't know what to say. It was so awful! There had been no slaves in Miller's Forks, and none on Stoney Creek. Even here where some people had slaves, the Armstrong household had none, for Hester Starkey was a hired servant, not a slave. How would it feel to belong to a master, to have to do whatever he said, no matter what?

"My little boy was so scared when they tore him out of my arms and forced him on that wagon!" Marcus went on. "And Dulcie was hugging him to her, trying to comfort him, with that hopeless look in her eyes like she had died inside. That look is burned into my brain like a brand, Miss Sarah. I don't reckon I'll ever forget it to my dying day. My Dulcie could sing like an angel, but I've often wondered if she's sung a note since that terrible morning."

Sarah felt tears stinging her eyes. "I'm so sorry, Marcus. I just don't understand how anyone can own someone else, anyway. Don't we all just belong to God?"

He smiled, and began walking again, this time toward the gates. "You know that, Miss Sarah, and I know it, but some people take for themselves what rightfully ain't theirs to take."

He sighed deeply. "Since then, I've looked, and I've sent word. Colonel Armstrong has tried to locate them. Governor Henry has tried. I think he would buy them and bring them back here for me. But it seems they've dropped off the face of the earth without a trace."

"I'm so sorry," she said again.

"Well, it's been a long time, Miss Sarah. I reckon my little Samuel would be a big boy by now. And ole Marcus has learned to live day by day with his grief pushed down to where it's bearable. The good Lord won't put on us more than we can bear, if we just trust Him to help carry the burden."

He stood lost in thought for a few moments. "These gardens are my family now, missy. I was so glad Governor Henry asked me to come back to work here after he moved into the palace. He's a kindly man, and a fair one. The minute he rode into town and found me in those stocks today, he demanded I be set free." He chuckled. "I'm not likely to see anybody as angry as he was, not twice in one lifetime!"

Suddenly, light touched his dark eyes. "I know where I've seen you before, Miss Sarah!" he exclaimed. "In the Armstrong pew with your aunt and cousins at Bruton Parish Church!"

She looked puzzled. "But I haven't seen you at church, Marcus."

He chuckled. "And you're not likely to! Folks like me—free or slave—sit up in the north balcony."

They had reached the gates, and Sarah slipped through them. Then she was surprised to see him do the same, and turn to lock the gates behind them. She had assumed he lived there on the palace grounds, but he walked with her toward Nicholson Street.

"Don't forget what I said, now, missy," he said when they reached the Armstrong house. "These are uncertain times, and you never know when you might need a friend, even such an unlikely one as ole Marcus!" Chuckling, he walked on to Botetourt Street and turned north.

"Good night!" she called after him. "I won't forget!"

"It's about time you got back, missy!" Hester Starkey said from the doorway. "I was about to lock you out!"

Sarah smiled up at her, thinking how different Hester was from Marcus. Surely she hadn't faced such tragedy as his. Yet she was as bitter as a green persimmon before the frost turned it mellow. And Marcus was . . . well, not exactly happy, Sarah supposed, but at least content.

She wished she could be more like him, but it seemed she was always wanting something she couldn't have. In Kentucky, she had wanted to be back in Virginia. In Virginia, she wanted to be with her family in Kentucky. And if she were back in Kentucky, what would she want then?

5

Sarah woke to singing birds, the sweet scent of Aunt Charity's pale pink roses carried into the bedroom on a soft summer breeze, and the tantalizing smell of pancakes cooking. She knew it was early. The air wasn't hot yet, and the sun was just peeking over the windowsill. Careful not to touch Abigail, she rolled over on her back and stretched until her toes touched the footboard.

Then she remembered. Today was Sunday, and her new blue dress was ready to wear to church. But even that exciting prospect was overshadowed by the fact that they began their lessons tomorrow morning with their new tutor!

"She seems genteel and learned," Aunt Charity had announced over supper a few nights ago, "and I've engaged Miss Gordon's services as a tutor for the three of you for four weeks. At the end of that time, we will evaluate your progress and decide about further lessons."

Sarah hugged herself in anticipation. How grand it

would be to see Gabrielle again, to introduce her to Tabitha and Abigail, to listen to her charming French accent as she instructed them in the skills young ladies needed to survive in these busy modern times!

First, though, there was Sunday and the new blue dress to experience. Sarah rolled over and off the edge of the featherbed onto her feet. She held her breath as the tall bedstead creaked, but Abigail just turned over onto her stomach, stuck one arm up under the plump feather pillow, and began to breathe deeply again. Sarah knew the other girls would have to get up soon, but she relished these early morning moments alone.

Sarah poured a small amount of water from the pitcher into the bowl and quickly washed her face. She replaced her white nightdress with her new blue dress, and covered it with one of the white aprons Aunt Charity insisted the girls wear to keep their dresses clean. Then she tiptoed from the room, sat down on the top step, and pulled on her shoes and stockings.

Her thoughts on Gabrielle and the glorious mornings ahead, Sarah had the table set for breakfast and was helping Hester carry food into the dining room when Aunt Charity came in and took her place at the end of the table. Sarah was rewarded for her efforts by a rare, approving smile from her aunt as they listened to her cousins stumble, half asleep, down the stairs to join them for breakfast.

Then they were bustling about, Abigail bewailing the fact that she couldn't find the ribbons that matched her pink dress. She accused first Sarah, and then Megan of taking them. "If I can't have a new dress to wear, it seems I could at least have hair ribbons to match my old one!" she whined to Tabitha.

★ Chapter Five ★

Tabitha, dressing contentedly even without the benefit of a new frock, was dreaming of seeing Seth Coler at church and hardly noticed Abigail's tantrum.

Aunt Charity noticed, though, and quickly put an end to it. "Here are your ribbons, Abigail, in the dresser drawer where you put them the last time you wore them," she said sharply. "And you owe Sarah and Megan an apology, young lady!"

"Sorry," Abigail muttered sulkily, adjusting her ribbons.

Sarah ignored her, and went on brushing Megan's curls.

"You look beautiful, 'Gail!" Meggie comforted her sister. "And your dress isn't so very old, 'cause I remember you got it to wear to the Randolph's party just before Sarah came."

Abigail glared at her, and flounced out of the room with a rustle of pink silk. Sarah supposed Abigail was still upset because Sarah had a new dress and Abigail didn't. But Abigail knew Sarah hadn't had anything but rough linsey-woolsey for over a year. Anyway, her jealousy didn't give her any reason to be rude to Megan.

Sarah gave the sad-looking little girl a quick hug. "You look beautiful yourself, Miss Meggie," she said, taking her hand and swinging it between them as they followed the rest of the family out the door and down the street to church.

The church bells sounded the call to worship as Sarah entered the Armstrong pew behind Abigail. Megan, last in line, closed the door to the four-foot wooden walls that surrounded the family pew. Sarah could look up and see the rector in his pulpit high on their right, but sitting down, she could see only the tops of people's heads in the closed pews around them.

Remembering Marcus's comment the night before, she searched the north balcony on her left, but could not distinguish his face from among other dark faces up there.

Sarah spread the skirts of her new dress over the red cushion, and turned to smile at Abigail out of the joy of being alive.

Abigail rolled her blue eyes and turned to watch the organist and his assistant take their places down front, where the pipes of the organ rose tall and straight to the vaulted ceiling. Then, feeling superior in her knowledge, she nudged Sarah and whispered, "That's Peter Pelham, the gaoler. I used to take harpsichord lessons from him."

"The gaoler?" Sarah whispered back in surprise.

"Yes, but he's a much better musician than he is a gaoler. He gets drunk and lets prisoners escape. Pa says he may have to be removed someday. But he needs the job." She nodded toward a front pew where a woman followed by many children was being seated. "That's his wife, Ann, and the survivors of their fourteen children."

Sarah watched until the Pelhams crowded into their pew and shut the door, then she turned her attention to the gray-haired man seated at the organ. "Who's that with him?" she whispered to Abigail.

Abigail shrugged. "Oh, just one of his prisoners. He brings one almost every Sunday to pump the organ for him."

"Girls!" Aunt Charity warned them to be quiet with a harsh whisper.

Sarah settled back in the seat, prepared to listen to the rector's sermon, but it was long and dry. Finally she gave up and let her eyes roam around the building, taking in what she could see of it above the pew walls. Abigail said the

walls were to keep them warm in the winter in the unheated church.

Finally the service was over, and they filed out to the churchyard, where Abigail met some friends, and Tabitha stood watching for Seth Coler to leave the building with Josiah Chowning and his family. Apparently, Seth lived with the Chownings.

Standing against the brick wall that surrounded the churchyard, Sarah saw the girl who had sold her the tin cup of apple juice. She smiled, and the girl smiled back, showing her missing tooth. Sarah realized she didn't know the girl's name. She walked past scattered white gravestones to where she stood beside a raised, flat tombstone.

"I'm Sarah Moore," she said. "I'm from Kentucky, but I'm staying with . . ."

"Colonel Armstrong's family," the girl finished.

"Everybody knows that! I'm Betsy, and I'm indentured to the Chownings."

"Indentured?" Sarah repeated. "What's that?"

Betsy laughed, again showing the gap where her tooth had been. "That means the Chownings paid my passage over here from Ireland, and I have to work for them until I pay them back. I was ten when I came, and my contract's for seven years, so I've only got five more to go!"

The girl had been a servant at the tavern since she was ten years old, and she would be seventeen before she was free! It sounded like a hard life to Sarah, but Betsy didn't seem daunted by it. "I had a friend named Betsy once," Sarah said, changing the subject.

Betsy smiled her contagious, gap-toothed smile. "Have you still got your pretty little tin cup?"

"Yes, I do," Sarah said. "I have it hidden in a safe place."

"There are no safe places anymore," the girl said sadly. "My brother's gone off to the army, and all we hear from the men congregating at the tavern is war, war, war! Seth Coler too! I look for him to take off to join the army any day! I ain't no Tory, but I wish this blasted war was over!"

"I have a brother fighting up north somewhere," Sarah said sympathetically, "and I wish it were over too!"

"Sarah, it's time to go!" Aunt Charity called, motioning for her to join them.

Betsy smiled. "They don't want you hobnobbing with the likes o' me," she said, with a sassy grin. She leaned closer, "Bet she won't let you come near Chowning's, neither!" Betsy walked off to follow the Chownings out the gate, leaving Sarah standing there with her mouth open.

"You can't associate with the servants of Williamsburg,

Sarah!" Abigail scolded as they walked home. "You have embarrassed us all to no end!"

"Did you see your sister standing there dreaming over Seth Coler? Isn't he a servant of the Chownings?" Sarah replied.

Abigail stared at her, then picked up her skirts and swished them haughtily. "Seth is an apprentice, not a servant," she said. "He works to learn a trade. He may not make much money now, but he will own a tavern someday. And, if Tabitha has anything to do with it, it will be a respectable place to take your family for a meal. Of course, he wouldn't suit me," she went on, "but Tabby has no higher ambitions, so let her have him! Me, I've got bigger fish to fry!"

"Have you got him picked out, yet, Abigail?" Sarah asked. "And does he know he's destined for the frying pan?"

"Him?" Abigail snapped, glaring at her. "I plan to own things in my own right. I won't depend on some husband to tell me what I can have and what I can't have! Maybe I'll own a milliner's shop, like Gabrielle Gordon," she went on, "or a jeweler's shop like the Golden Ball. And I'll have indentured servants working for me! How do you like that, Cousin Sarah?"

"I still don't see why I can't be friends with Betsy," Sarah said doggedly. "She seems nice, and she has the friendliest smile I've ever seen. Anyway, didn't you hear what the rector said this morning about God loving the world so much that He gave his only begotten Son so that whosoever believeth on Him should not perish, but have eternal life?"

Abigail stared at her blankly. "What's that got to do with Betsy?"

"Well, what if Betsy believes in Jesus? Will you and Aunt Charity stick your noses in the air and walk right past her on the streets of heaven without so much as a 'good morning,' just because she once was a servant?"

"Don't be ridiculous, Sarah!" Abigail snapped, picking up her skirts and hurrying to catch up with her mother and sisters.

She never did answer my question, Sarah thought. It was hard to understand how some people felt about other human beings, who, except for circumstances they could not control, were just like them. What was it that Uncle Ethan had framed and hanging on the parlor wall? "We hold these truths to be self-evident, that all men are created equal."

Would Uncle Ethan pass Betsy by too? He was a part of the freedom movement, but he was a Virginian, just like Aunt Charity and Abigail.

Sarah remembered the way people from all backgrounds had mingled in Kentucky. Station in life didn't seem to matter when your life depended on the marksmanship of the person next to you in the fort, or on some former servant's willingness to share with you when you ran out of supplies.

"I reckon I'm more of a Kentuckian than I thought!" Sarah said aloud. She met Abigail's raised eyebrows with a grin every bit as sassy as Betsy's.

★ 6 ★

Each evening since Aunt Charity had announced her arrangement with the tutor, Sarah had taken a walk down Nicholson to where it joined Waller Street. She had stood there, staring at the milliner's front door, willing it to open.

"Why are we standing here watching that brown house?" Megan had asked on one of the evenings Sarah had not been able to escape the house without her. "You said we would catch fireflies on the Palace Green, Sarah," she had added, tugging at Sarah's hand impatiently. And reluctantly, Sarah had let the little girl lead her back the way they had come, toward the street in front of the Governor's Palace.

One evening, though, the blue door to the brown house had opened, and Gabrielle had come out. She stood a moment on the front stoop, her white dress fluffed out around her like a giant althea blossom. Her dark, coppery hair picked up a faint glow from the young moon as she turned and said something to someone inside the house. In a moment, she was joined by a gentleman who took her arm and guided her down the walk.

"Is that her, Sarah?" Megan asked excitedly. "Your new tootler?"

"Shhh!" Sarah had cautioned, and they had watched until the couple disappeared into the shadows past Christiana Campbell's Tavern. Then she had turned to Megan and hugged her. "Yes, that's our new tutor. Isn't she beautiful?"

Megan's nod was barely visible to Sarah in the growing dusk. "Who's that man with her, Sarah? Is that her husband?"

Sarah shook her head uncertainly. "I don't know, Meggie. I don't think she has a husband."

"Maybe he's her free-and-say! Tabby lives for the day when she can have a free-and-say."

Sarah laughed and tousled the little girl's curls. "Fiancé," she corrected. "And Tabitha lives for the day she can marry Seth Coler. I think she'd skip the whole engagement process if Aunt Charity would let her. And if Seth were willing!" she added.

"Well, then, maybe he's just a gentleman collar. I heard Ma say that Miz Barne's daughter had a gentleman collar last Sunday. What's a gentleman collar, anyway, Sarah?" Megan asked seriously.

"Gentleman 'caller,' Meggie! What in the world am I going to do with you?" she said, laughing again. Then she turned to look back to where Gabrielle had disappeared in the darkness. "But anybody as lovely as Gabrielle Gordon may have a dozen gentlemen callers, I suppose," she sighed, taking Megan's hand and starting home.

★ Chapter Six ★

Most evenings, though, as Sarah watched from the corner, the milliner—if she came out at all—either walked alone over to Christiana Campbell's and disappeared inside, or she walked on down around the corner toward the other taverns.

Now, the day had finally come when they would be going to her house for lessons! Sarah was up and dressed before Tabitha and Abigail had even stirred. Either they had forgotten about today, she decided, or it didn't mean as much to them as it did to her.

Sarah had thought of little else since Aunt Charity had announced her arrangement with the tutor, and she could hardly contain herself now through breakfast and morning chores.

Finally, Aunt Charity called them into the parlor and began to give them instructions. They must not talk to strangers; they must go straight to the milliner's; they must not walk on the side of the street in front of the gaol; and, above all, they must not say anything at all about Mr. Armstrong's comings and goings.

Having assured her they would commit none of these unpardonable sins, the three girls set off together for Waller Street and their first morning of being tutored by Gabrielle Gordon.

"I want to hear all about the latest fashions from Paris, and I want to learn some French words that my friends won't understand," Abigail planned.

"Oh, 'Gail, you mustn't show off so!" Tabitha scolded. "I want to learn how to run a proper household, accounts and everything. And how to give a dinner party. And how to write proper formal invitations."

"Aunt Charity could teach you all those things, Tabby,"

Sarah broke in. "Don't you want to know about the big world out there? About cities like Paris, where Gabrielle is from, or Philadelphia or Boston, where your pa goes so often but won't say a word about them?"

"Not really," Tabitha answered seriously. "I just want to know . . ."

". . . how to capture and tame the wild and wonderful Seth Coler!" Abigail intoned sarcastically, with one hand held daintily out to her side, and the other holding her skirts as she curtsied deeply. "That's all you think about, Tabitha Armstrong. I declare, you make me absolutely ill!"

Tabitha just smiled serenely, crossed the street to obey Aunt Charity's orders about passing the gaol, and walked on around the corner.

"Why is your mother so afraid for us to walk past the gaol?" Sarah asked Abigail. "Isn't Peter Pelham the gaoler? We see him every Sunday playing the organ at Bruton Parish Church."

"Yes," Abigail answered, "but as Hester says, 'He has a fondness for the wine when it is red in the cup.' Too many prisoners under his care have escaped."

Sarah recalled the hard-looking man who had accompanied the gaoler to church last Sunday. She shivered, and quickly crossed the street.

Tabitha was waiting for them at the end of Waller Street. "You already know her, Sarah," she said. "You go first and introduce us."

All at once, Sarah felt her strength drain right out through her feet. What would she say? Would she be as tongue-tied as she had been the day she met Gabrielle?

Just then, the door to the milliner's shop opened, and Gabrielle appeared on the stoop. "Ah, *chérie*, you are here!"

she exclaimed. "And you have brought the charming Armstrong cousins! Welcome! Come in, and let us get acquainted."

Awkwardly, Sarah made the introductions, and the girls followed their new tutor inside the house. Gabrielle led them through the crowded shop into a parlor behind it, where they saw four chairs grouped around a small, round table set for tea.

Sarah knew from the looks on their faces that her cousins were as enchanted with the room and its delicate furnishings as she was. From the graceful folds of the curtains to the white tablecloth trimmed with the curtains' dainty flowered fabric, to the small enameled gold and white clock on the mantel, the room was as elegant and charming as its owner.

"Come, *mesdemoiselles,* let us sit down and learn the proper way to prepare and serve a tea, *non?*" She waved a graceful hand toward the curved chairs around the table, and Sarah set the example by obeying instantly.

Soon, all three girls were old hands at serving a proper tea, except for pouring hot tea from the flowered pot into the matching cups.

"The trick is to do it gracefully, but keep up an interesting conversation so that the act of pouring is hardly noticed. And never, never allow a drop to spill," Gabrielle cautioned. "That is the ultimate faux pas, *chérie!*" she told Abigail, who hastened to dab with a napkin at a small wet spot forming under the spout.

"Ah, don't worry," Gabrielle laughed softly at their looks of dismay, for each of them had been guilty of the so-called "faux pas." "We shall practice many, many times. And when we are finished, you will be the most gracious hostesses in all of America! Just like the admirable and indomitable Charity Armstrong, your mother and aunt. I promise!"

She glanced at the clock, and rose from her chair. "It is nearly time for the noonday meal, and Madame Armstrong made it very clear that you would be expected home for that. So our lessons are over for the day. I will see all of you tomorrow morning, *oui?*"

"Oh, yes, ma'am," they chorused, rising hastily and moving toward the door.

Abigail barely waited until the door shut behind them before exclaiming, "What a beautiful creature! What elegant airs and movements she has! How graceful! I think I'll do my hair like hers. And I wonder what Ma would say if I painted my nails?"

"She'd skin you alive," Tabitha answered, "so get the thought out of your mind!" She sighed. "She is lovely, isn't she? And what taste she uses in decorating her home! I hope she will teach us how she does it!"

Sarah nodded, already grieving over having to share her precious Gabrielle. She wanted to keep Gabrielle all to herself. Sarah wasn't worried about Tabitha. She only coveted a close relationship with Seth Coler. But, likely as not, Abigail would push her way between them, taking more than her fair share of Gabrielle, as she did of everything else.

Still, Aunt Charity wasn't likely to have let her come for tutoring by herself, especially since Abigail and Tabitha needed a tutor also.

Oh, well, Sarah thought, as they neared the Armstrong house. She would just make the best of it and take advantage of any opportunity to be alone with Gabrielle.

★ Chapter Six ★

And she vowed she would be the best pupil Gabrielle had ever known.

In no time, it seemed, the four weeks were up, and Aunt Charity tested their newly acquired skills.

"I am pleased," she said at last. "You have learned a great deal in a short time. We will continue your tutoring with Miss Gordon."

Sarah let out the breath she had been holding, joined hands with Tabitha and Abigail, and they danced happily around the room.

"Girls! Girls!" Aunt Charity's voice cut through their merriment. "You will cause me to change my mind!"

Sarah dropped instantly into a chair, but Abigail, with a saucy grin, protested, "But it's a new dance our tutor taught us!"

Aunt Charity smiled a thin smile, then went on with plans for future lessons. "I want to change your schedule from morning to afternoon, if that is agreeable with Miss Gordon. Your being away at the busiest time of the day is working a hardship on Hester and me."

She turned to Tabitha and Abigail. "You know your father has decided that money we once used to hire extra help can better be used for . . ." she hesitated, ". . . for another purpose. And with two such capable young ladies in the house—and now three, with you here Sarah—he is right, I am sure." She stood up. "Sarah, run down and tell Miss Gordon that you won't be there this morning, but I will call on her this afternoon to arrange a new schedule."

Then she addressed Abigail and Tabitha again. "While Hester and I turn some of those blackberries in the kitchen into jam, you can air and tidy the bedrooms. In fact, there isn't a room in this house that doesn't need sweeping and dusting!" she said, as she went briskly into the kitchen. "And hurry back, Sarah," she called. "I'm sure they can use your help!"

Sarah exchanged a look of resignation with Abigail, as Tabitha hurried to get the dust cloths and beeswax for polishing the furniture.

"Tabby is definitely a candidate for Williamsburg's mental hospital!" Abigail whispered. "She actually likes housework!"

"She'll clean all morning, dreaming about keeping her own house, with Seth Coler in it!" Sarah whispered back, giggling.

"Girls, I assume you know the carpet sweeper is in the closet under the stairs and the broom is here in the kitchen," Aunt Charity prompted. "You can do the upstairs first, before it gets too hot up there."

Abigail rolled her eyes and headed for the closet, as Sarah, still smiling, left the house.

Sarah wanted to run all the way to Waller Street, but the hot July sun convinced her to walk by the second block. She stopped on the stoop of the brown house to wipe perspiration from her brow and straighten her apron. Then she pushed against the latch of the blue door and walked into the milliner's shop, the bell jingling over the door.

"Gabrielle!" she called, walking straight through the shop and into the parlor, as they did for lessons each weekday.

A man jumped up hastily from the round table, spilling tea on the white cloth. Sarah noted that their tea table was now set for breakfast, as she grabbed a napkin and began dabbing at the widening stain.

"I'm so sorry!" she almost whispered. "I didn't know Gabrielle had . . . I didn't mean to . . ." She stopped in confusion. Slowly, she raised her eyes and was startled by

the intensity of the pale blue gaze that met hers.

"I am Gabrielle's cousin, Alistair," he explained, reaching for her hand and bowing over it. His blond mustache tickled as it brushed her knuckles. "And you must be Gabrielle's star pupil I have been hearing so much about this morning," he said with a smile that did not reach the cold, pale eyes. "Miss Armstrong, is it?"

"Moore," she corrected. "Sarah Moore. Charity Armstrong is my aunt. Where's Gabrielle?" She suddenly felt uncomfortable talking with this strange man alone in Gabrielle's parlor.

Just then, Gabrielle entered the room carrying a small tray which held a covered bowl and a silver-topped glass jar filled with red jelly.

"Well, Alistair, the bread is just right, and this is the last of the currant jelly. Oh, Sarah!" she gasped. "I did not expect you so early!" She stopped in confusion, a frown creasing her forehead and a flush mounting her cheeks. Her gaze darted from one to the other.

"I have introduced myself to your pupil, Gabrielle, and explained that I am your cousin, here on a brief visit to the colonies," the man put in smoothly.

Gabrielle laughed nervously. "But we are no longer colonies, Alistair!" she chided, setting the tray on the table. "We are the United States of America, fighting for the freedom to make our own rules and regulations." Her eyes never left Sarah's face.

"Forgive me, ladies." He gave a slight bow. I have only been in the colonies . . . in America for a few days, and it is my first visit to your delightful Virginia. You must give me time to get accustomed to your new government and its terminology."

Gabrielle patted his arm. "We will allow you that one small error, cousin! But no more!" she admonished, shaking her finger under his nose.

She turned to Sarah. "But what are you doing here so early, *chérie?* Is something wrong? Our four weeks are up. Is Madame Armstrong not pleased with your progress? Has she decided to cancel our arrangement?" There was an anxious look in her eyes.

"Oh, no, Gabrielle!" Sarah hastened to explain. "She is very pleased. But she wants me to ask you to excuse us this morning. She will call on you this afternoon, if that is convenient for you, to make arrangements to continue our tutoring at a new time next week."

Gabrielle looked relieved, and Sarah wondered if the money was so important to her. Perhaps the millinery shop did not bring in enough to live on, with the competition from the older shop on Duke of Gloucester, as well as some from John Greenhow's store.

"Very good, *chérie*. Tell Madame Armstrong I shall await her visit with pleasure, and I will hope to see you, Abigail, and Tabitha next week."

Sarah knew she had been dismissed. She curtsied, then turned and left the room, and the shop. Only after she was out on the stoop did she remember the lesson Gabrielle had taught them about always responding to an introduction by expressing pleasure at making the person's acquaintance. She felt her cheeks flush with embarrassment. What a dolt Gabrielle must think her star pupil was, to shame her in front of her cousin, and after she had praised her to him!

Sarah stood on the stoop uncertainly. Should she go back inside and correct her faux pas, as Gabrielle would call it? Or should she go on home and hope they hadn't noticed? But Gabrielle would have noticed! She was sure of that!

Sarah turned to reenter the shop. Then she heard the man say, "It is perfect, Gabrielle! There won't be the close family allegiance of the others to overcome, and it is obvious she adores you. She will do anything you ask."

"I do not like it, Alistair," Gabrielle answered in a voice so soft Sarah had to strain to hear the words. ". . . using someone who trusts me . . ." Her words faded away.

The man's laugh was short and harsh. "It is all part of the game, my dear," he said. "All part of this deadly game we play."

Sarah turned and ran all the way back to the house on Nicholson Street, where she joined her cousins at their housekeeping chores without a word.

By eleven o'clock, the upstairs rooms were neat and dust free. Even little Megan, with some help from Sarah, had cleaned her own room. Then the girls descended on the downstairs rooms, with their mops and pails and dust cloths.

"You do the parlor, Abigail. Sarah, you do Pa's study. I'll tackle the dining room and all its dusty china!" Tabitha assigned, already on her way.

Sarah opened the study door, breathing in the musty odor of books and old leather, mingled with the wax from the candle on her uncle's big walnut desk. One side of the room was filled, floor to ceiling, with bookshelves.

As she ran the dust mop over the floor, around the deep red rugs with the hunting scenes dyed into them, Sarah noticed on the opposite wall, a frame holding a paper filled with words. She moved over to get a closer look, and saw that the words were surrounded by a sketch of a cedar tree with an eagle perched on its top branch. It was the same puzzling design that was on the tin cup that now lay hidden in her travel bag upstairs.

The paper said the verses were from Ezekiel 17. She repeated the words as she read:

Thus saith the Lord God; A great eagle with great wings . . . took the highest branch of the cedar . . . he placed it by great waters. . . .

Thus saith the Lord God; I will also take of the highest branch of the high cedar, and will set it . . . and it shall bring forth boughs, and bear fruit, and be a goodly cedar: and under it shall dwell all fowl of every wing. . . .

And all the trees of the field shall know that I the Lord have brought down the high tree, have exalted the low tree, have dried up the green tree, and have made the dry tree to flourish.

What do those verses mean? Sarah wondered, as she dusted the bookshelves. *Why does Uncle Ethan have them framed and hanging on his study wall?* She promised herself she would ask him when he came home.

By noon, the sweeping and dusting were done, and Aunt Charity had inspected their work.

"Very good, girls," she commended as she came back into the kitchen. "Now, set the table, and we will have a bite of cold lunch. Hester and I are too busy to stop to cook right now." And they sat down to cold leftovers from last night's roast, and slices of bread from a crusty loaf left from that week's baking day. They finished off the meal with the rare treat of a bowl of Hester's blackberries topped with sugar and cream.

"You haven't said three words all morning, Sarah," Megan chided as they gathered the dishes and put them beside the tub of water sitting in the dry sink. "I do believe the cat's got your tongue!"

Sarah made a grab for Megan's tongue with her thumb and forefinger. "Then I'll just have to take yours, I guess!" she said, chasing the little girl out the back door and into the garden.

Laughing, Megan ran around the flower beds, crawled under the fence, and ran through the fields where the Armstrong cattle, sheep, and horses grazed. Sarah started to go after her, but the animals seemed gentle enough, and her heart wasn't really in the chase.

She sat down under the cedar tree, her thoughts still troubled by the conversation she had overheard between Gabrielle and her cousin. What on earth could they have meant? The soft breeze through the cedar branches above her head seemed to whisper a warning, but she couldn't quite grasp its meaning.

She got up and walked around the house, where she saw Aunt Charity, her basket over her arm, going out the front gate. She headed up Nicholson, then turned toward Duke of Gloucester Street. Sarah knew she would complete her shopping, then visit Gabrielle to make arrangements for further lessons.

Sarah waited a moment, then followed along Nicholson, turning in the opposite direction once she reached the Palace Green. Quickly, she passed through the open palace gates and crossed the ballroom gardens. She skirted the maze, and came out into the lower gardens, where flower beds added happy color to the greens and browns of the grass and trees.

She sat down on the bridge at the north end of the canal, remembering the journey to Kentucky. Sarah would take off her shoes and stockings and dabble her hot, tired feet in a stream whenever Pa would let them rest a moment. The water was too far below the bridge for dabbling today, though.

What was her family doing on this hot July day? The crops would be laid by until harvesttime. Ma, like Aunt Charity, might be preserving berries, if she had any sweetener. Pa was likely building a new shed or fence, or maybe a new room on the cabin. Luke might be helping Pa, or swimming with the Larkin boys. And little Jamie would be running around, getting in everybody's way.

How I miss them! Sarah thought. Just a few short months ago, she was in Kentucky pining for her former home in Miller's Forks, Virginia. She had vowed she'd never be a Kentuckian, that she would find a way to return to Virginia someday. Now, here she was in Virginia, longing for the cramped log cabin back on the banks of Stoney Creek.

Sarah thought about the big log room where they cooked, ate, and slept. She pictured the rough wooden table with its scars from the Indians' tomahawks which had nearly scalped Ma. She could see the crude wooden bowls and utensils they had to use.

Then she thought of Aunt Charity's elegant dining room with its rich dark furniture and soft carpet. She thought of her aunt's polished, glass-front china cabinet, and felt her resentment rise at the thought of Grandma's china sitting there. Grandma had willed it to Ma, and Ma should have it. Aunt Charity had been willed the harpsichord.

Sarah wished her ma could have all the nice things she had left behind in Virginia. She wished Pa could have the tools and supplies he needed. She wished Luke and Jamie could go to a good school like the boys' school here in Williamsburg.

Pa always had answered her longings with the promise of "someday." Someday Kentucky would have hard-packed dirt roads like Virginia's. Someday there would be brick houses instead of log cabins. Someday there would be shops and schools and churches.

Well, maybe I will just stay here in Williamsburg until "someday"! she thought. But she missed her family so much, especially Ma. And she missed little Jamie, toddling after her, yelling, "Wait, Sadie! Jamie go too?"

Here she had Megan following everywhere she went. She had never had a younger sister, and she had grown very fond of her little cousin. Unlike everybody else in the Armstrong household, little Meggie seemed to think everything Sarah did was perfect.

"It's perfect. She will do anything you ask." The man's

words came back to haunt her, along with Gabrielle's almost whispered response, "I hate using someone who trusts me."

Sarah pushed the troubling thoughts aside, determined not to let the mysterious conversation between Gabrielle and her cousin spoil her joy in being with her friend, in continuing their lessons together.

Now, though, Megan would be wondering where she was, and why she had stopped playing their game. It was time she headed back home.

Not home, she reminded herself, getting up from her perch above the canal and brushing off her skirt. If she had learned anything from her trip back to Virginia, it was that home is not a house. Home is where people who love you live.

Sarah sighed, suddenly feeling very lonely.

8

As the long summer days moved slowly past, and the thick dust gathered in the streets and on the thirsty gardens, Sarah felt that she had learned all the social graces she cared to know, and more about running a household than she wanted to know.

She, Abigail, and Tabitha had also studied a little geography and history, and Gabrielle had assigned them books to read from Uncle Ethan's library. Tabitha had spent several weeks on one book that Sarah had read in two days, and Abigail simply refused to read anything that didn't have something to do with fashion or playing the harpsichord or dancing.

One afternoon, Gabrielle sent a note to Aunt Charity, asking if Sarah could come back and study an hour or so after supper three days each week, at least while the days were long enough for her to get home before dark. Sarah held her breath until Aunt Charity agreed.

"I certainly don't envy you, Sarah!" Abigail said spitefully, as Sarah prepared to go back to Gabrielle's for her first private lesson. "I love the fashion and music lessons, but Latin? And who knows what else she'll expect you to study! You'll end up with awful headaches!"

After a lesson in Latin and one in world history, tutor and pupil sat drinking spiced tea, and Gabrielle commented, "You did very well with these harder subjects, Sarah. I am pleased. But I knew you would. You are so different from your cousins." She sipped her tea, absorbed in thought, while Sarah hugged the compliment to herself.

"Tabitha is like my old tabby cat over there," Gabrielle mused, looking at the gray and yellow cat dozing on the hearth. "She will always be content to sit on her own hearth and purr over her own things and people. But she makes up for her lack of interest in literature and the world by her near perfection in all the household skills."

Sarah hoped she would not pursue that topic, for her own crooked stitches and hard, flat bread fell far short of Tabitha's standards.

"And our Abigail," Gabrielle continued, "is like the alley cat, I think. She's not opposed to using her claws to get what she wants. But she is adept at fashion, and intent on grooming her own fur. She is as graceful as a cat, too, and excels in the music and the dance."

"What am I, Gabrielle?" Sarah questioned, eager for compliments of her own. "Am I, too, some kind of cat?"

"Well, *chérie*, you are like a cat in your lively curiosity. But I think, maybe, you are the wild cat, having come from the untamed Kentucky, and being so determined to do things your own way."

"Is that bad?" Sarah asked, uncertain that she had

received the compliment she craved.

"Oh, *non, chérie!*" Gabrielle answered. "I hear this is the way of the wild Kentuckians—very stubborn, but very brave, and determined to be free at any cost!" She smiled and came over to give her a brief hug. "You are the best of all, you know. My star pupil."

The words brought back the memory of Gabrielle's cousin, but refusing to let the cold Alistair intrude into their comfortable companionship, Sarah asked, "And you, Gabrielle? What kind of cat are you?"

The tutor gave that some thought, then answered with a saucy grin, "I think, perhaps, I am not a cat. I am the fox, *chérie,* wily and cunning, and not very well loved by those who keep the chicken coop."

"I don't understand, Gabrielle," Sarah said. When the other woman did not respond, she went on, "I don't think you are like the fox, anyway, except maybe for your copper-colored hair and eyes, and the graceful way you walk. But surely everyone loves you! Even those who have chicken coops!"

Gabrielle smiled sadly. "You would be surprised, then, *chérie.* But it is this war, perhaps. It has everyone's nerves on edge. I can see why your family moved to Kentucky! Your father is a wise man."

"But Pa did not move to Kentucky to escape the war," Sarah said. "He wanted to claim new land. The war had not touched us in Miller's Forks, except that my brother Nate joined the army. And he got that idea here in Williamsburg, when he was in school. He was involved in the Sons of Liberty. He heard the fiery speeches of Patrick Henry."

"Ah, *oui!* The Governor Henry with his, 'Caesar had his Brutus, Oliver his Cromwell, and George the Third . . . may profit by their example!' They say excited Patriots and disturbed Tories rioted in the taverns the day he uttered those words." Gabrielle sat in thought a moment, then sighed. "Most of the Tories are gone now," she said.

Sarah frowned. Why did it matter? The fewer Tories, the better!

"Nate says Mr. Henry also told the General Assembly, 'I know not what course others may take, but as for me, give me liberty or give me death!' " She laughed. "I guess Kentuckians and Virginians are a lot alike," she added.

"That was two years ago, and yet they all still follow their feisty governor like so many sheep," Gabrielle said scornfully. "Peyton Randolph, Richard Henry Lee, Benjamin Waller, Tom Jefferson, even George Wythe, the most scholarly and learned man in Virginia!—all march behind Henry, playing their war games like little boys!"

That wasn't the way Nate had described it to Pa, Sarah recalled. "The Revolution is in the hearts of the people!" he had said. "Only God could stop it now, and He fights on our side!" But Sarah said nothing. She really didn't know enough about it to argue.

"I tell you, *ma petite*, I hate this war!" Gabrielle burst out. "The taverns are nothing but hotbeds of intrigue, of secret plans and whispered threats. And there are no more carefree parties and entertainments, only occasions to gather and talk more war! I do wish sometimes, *chérie*, that I had gone back to England with Governor Dunmore's family, and then back to France, where I belong!"

"Couldn't you still go?" Sarah asked. "It might be hard to get a ship to England these days, but surely there are some to France." She held her breath, knowing her heart would break if Gabrielle left Williamsburg, but she couldn't stand to see her so unhappy.

"*Non, chérie,* I cannot," she answered. "I . . . I have work to do here. Then, perhaps, when this awful war is over, I will go home."

Sarah let out her breath in relief. "I will go back to Kentucky someday too," she said. Maybe Gabrielle would be in Williamsburg as long as she was, she thought happily. But could her milliner's shop be so important that she must stay here when she obviously wanted to leave?

The tutor stood up. "Enough of this idle chatter," she said briskly. "Here are the assignments I have written out for you to complete before our next evening session. And I will see you and your cousins tomorrow afternoon."

Gabrielle walked Sarah to the door, and stood watching until she had turned the corner onto Nicholson Street. When Sarah glanced back, Gabrielle was walking quickly in the other direction, toward Christiana Campbell's Tavern.

Sarah walked slowly toward the Armstrong house, thinking of Gabrielle's words. What did she mean by her reference to "the chicken coop"? Almost everybody in Williamsburg had a chicken coop, and she had never heard anyone say they didn't like Gabrielle.

Oh, well, she thought as she saw Megan sitting on the front stoop, waiting for her, *sometimes I just don't understand Gabrielle.*

"I hate your evening lessons!" Megan blurted as she met Sarah at the gate. "I don't have anybody to play with when you go to the tootler's." Her mouth drew down into a pout.

Sarah gave the little girl a hug. "Go ask Aunt Charity if you can walk with me now, Meggie," she suggested. "We'll go down on the Green and catch fireflies."

★ Stranger in Williamsburg ★

As she waited, Sarah leaned on the gate, relishing the tangy fragrance of lavender and lemon balm from the flower beds behind the fence, mingled with the scent of wood smoke from the dying supper fires along Nicholson Street. The sun had painted the western horizon a deep rose color, and, in the east, she could see the faint outline of a pale slice of moon, accompanied by the evening star. Then somewhere, off beyond the town's limits, a whippoorwill called.

Sarah's thoughts flew back to the night she, Luke, and Pa had gone to take honey from a bee tree Luke had found in the forest. Suddenly Indians had surrounded them, calling to each other with the borrowed voices of whippoorwills. Since then, the plaintive cry always filled Sarah with dread.

She was glad for Megan's company when the little girl rejoined her, and they set off down the street in search of fireflies. Megan skipped every other step in her delight at being allowed to go.

"Sarah, will you be here with me always?" she asked suddenly, taking hold of her hand. "I've been thinking. If I missed you so much while you were just down the street at the tootler's, what would I do if you went away completely? You're my special friend!"

Sarah stopped and turned to face her. "Do you hear that whippoorwill, Meggie?" she asked. "There used to be a little brown whippoorwill that sat in the tree outside my bedroom window in Miller's Forks. I listened for his cry every evening, and it seemed he was telling me secrets no one else could understand. I thought of him as my very special friend, and I grieved over having to leave him when we moved to Kentucky. But you know what?" She swung the little girl's hand between them as they began to walk again.

"What?" Megan asked breathlessly.

"I found another whippoorwill just as special when we got to our new home." She thought it best not to mention the Indians.

Megan surprised her with her insight. "I'd never find another special friend like you, Sarah!" she insisted. "And if you went back to Kentucky, I think I would just curl up and die like that old woolly worm over there on that mounting block!"

Sarah followed the little girl's pointing finger to where a fuzzy, brown and gold worm lay curled into a ball in the ledge of the block the Peyton Randolph family used to mount their horses.

"You would not curl up and die, Megan Armstrong!" Sarah said. "You would go on growing up to be a beautiful young lady, and someday you would come visit me and stay as long as you liked."

"Could I really, Sarah? Could I visit you in Kentucky? Do you think Ma would let me?" She stopped at the corner of the street to look up into Sarah's eyes. "Do you really think I will grow up to be beautiful like you, Sarah?"

Sarah laughed. "Meggie, you will be much more beautiful than I will ever be. In fact, I think you're beautiful right now, with those big brown eyes like Uncle Ethan's and that curly hair like Aunt Charity's. My mother has that curly hair, too, and I never had a natural curl in my life! That's why I wear braids so much. They put a wave in my stick-straight hair."

Megan threw both arms around Sarah's waist and squeezed hard. "I love you, Sarah," she whispered.

"I love you, too, Meggie," Sarah answered, her mind

going back to Gabrielle's sad comment that "those who keep the chicken coop" loved her about as much as they did the fox. What could she have meant?

"Oh, Sarah, look at all the fireflies! Hurry! Let's catch some before their lights burn out!"

Chuckling, Sarah joined her little cousin in a mad chase after the tiny flashing lights.

Then the militia, in their buff-colored uniforms trimmed in red and blue, came marching down the street, smartly keeping time to the cadence of the drums. For a few moments, the two girls stood at the corner, watching the militia drill on the Palace Green. Sarah was surprised to see among them a familiar face. How long would it be before he, too, marched off to war, and John Greenhow's store would be minus one friendly, freckle-faced clerk?

This awful war has caused so many good things to end, Sarah thought sadly as she and Megan retraced their steps to the Armstrong house. How many more changes would it bring to their lives before it was over? How long before her brother, Nathan, could come home again? Or would he come home? Would he fall dead somewhere on some far-off battlefield? And Uncle Ethan? How long would it be before he could be home with his family all the time, instead of making short visits every few weeks?

And what on earth had Gabrielle meant by "those who keep the chicken coop"?

9

Sarah pushed against the latch of the blue door, but it did not open. She jiggled the latch. It appeared to be locked, but she had never known Gabrielle to lock her door. Of course, it was nearly past the hours of keeping shop.

"Who's there?" The voice came from behind the door; it was Gabrielle's.

"Gabrielle, it's me, Sarah. You told me to come back to study this evening. Remember?" She heard the latch slide back, and the door opened slightly.

"Come in, quickly!" Gabrielle commanded, grabbing her arm and pulling her inside. She pushed the door closed behind her, and slid the latch into place.

Alarm shot through Sarah. "What's wrong, Gabrielle? You never lock your door!"

Gabrielle laughed shakily. "But of course, I do, *chérie!* You have not been here so late before. It is not good for a young woman to leave her door unlatched at night, not in a town full of rowdy soldiers."

Sarah had to agree that the town had been full of militiamen lately. They seemed to drill up and down the streets and on the Palace Green all the time. Even now, in the distance, she could hear the steady beat of their drums and the shrill piping of the flutes.

"I need to ask a favor of you, *chérie*," Gabrielle said seriously. "A very important favor."

"Of course, Gabrielle. You know I will do anything I can for you." The words echoed through her memory from the day she had overheard the tutor talking with her cousin.

"My cousin, Alistair, is here again. But alas, someone has spread a nasty story about him so that he cannot come safely to my house. Nor can I be seen with him anywhere, for my own safety."

Sarah did not see what this cousin of Gabrielle's had to do with her. She did not like the Englishman with the cold, pale eyes.

"I'm sorry your cousin cannot visit you, Mademoiselle," she said, using one of the new terms they had learned. "But I do not see what that has to do with my lessons this evening. You did want me to come, didn't you?"

"Oh, *oui, chérie*, of course I did!" she answered quickly. "But I plan to let you go a little early tonight. And when you leave here, I need you to carry a message from me to Alistair."

"A message?" Sarah repeated, frowning. Then a feeling of dread came over her. "Gabrielle, you know I would do anything for you, but your cousin is British, and I cannot do anything to aid the British against my uncle and my brother. Please don't ask me!"

★ Chapter Nine ★

"*Chérie*, he is English, *oui*. But Alistair is a kind, gentle man who fights for no cause. He came to pick up a list of things I need so he could have them shipped to me from Paris. I cannot miss this chance to stock my shelves, Sarah. This awful war makes it so hard to get what I need." She sighed. "And now he has been caught in the middle of this desperate situation and been branded the *espion*—the spy!"

Sarah caught her breath at the ugly word.

"I assure you, *chérie*, it is a lie! Alistair is no more a spy than . . . than I am! And I cannot let him go without a word from me to show him that I know he is innocent, that I care!" She studied Sarah's expression, then added, "And, as I said, I need the supplies he can send me."

Sarah said nothing. She did not know what to say.

"Ah, well, if you do not trust me, I will have to find some other way," Gabrielle said sadly. "But you are about the only real friend I have here, and I . . ." Sarah was horrified to see her cover her eyes with both hands and begin to sob pitifully, her shoulders shaking under the soft pink silk of her dress.

"Don't cry, Gabrielle!" she blurted. "I will help you!" Sarah reached out hesitantly to pat her on the shoulder.

The woman turned and caught her in a quick embrace. "Oh, *mérci, chérie!* I knew I could count on you!" She stepped back, smiling now, and Sarah was relieved to see no hint of tears in the bright, dark eyes.

After Sarah had spent an hour conjugating Latin verbs, Gabrielle interrupted her work. "It is time, *chérie*. The evening fades, and Madame Armstrong will want you home before dark." She shoved a small note, sealed with blue sealing wax, into Sarah's apron pocket.

A pang of doubt shot through Sarah, but she pushed it

aside. Gabrielle had said he was innocent. What could it hurt to slip the man a list of supplies she needed for her shop? She had a hard time meeting the competition in Williamsburg as it was.

Gabrielle placed a manicured finger across her lips. "Not a word to anybody, *m'amie*. It would not do for either of us to be known as associates of my cousin, Alistair, the infamous British spy!" She laughed in the old way, and hugged Sarah. "Be careful, *chérie*. I am sure the niece of the Patriot Ethan Armstrong is in no danger from the militiamen. But discretion, as they say, is the better part of valor, is it not?"

"But where am I to find your cousin, Gabrielle?" Sarah asked, puzzled at the lack of directions.

Gabrielle gave her a little push toward the front door. "Oh, he will find you, *chérie*. Just walk down into the palace gardens, down by the end of the canal. But be careful, and remember, not a word to anyone! I will see you and the Armstrong cousins tomorrow—our contented old tabby cat and our little alley cat, *oui?*"

Hesitantly, Sarah opened the door.

"Oh, wait, *chérie!*" Gabrielle exclaimed. "I almost forgot! My tabby cat has a new litter of kittens. Would you like one? They are adorable, but I simply cannot keep them all." She led Sarah over to the hearth, where the old mother cat lay purring in a basket, with four soft bundles of fur asleep around her.

Sarah forced her thoughts away from spies and notes, and tried to concentrate on the kittens. She hadn't had a cat since she'd had to leave Tiger behind with her best friend, Martha Hutchinson, when they had moved to Kentucky. She had cried for days every time she thought of him.

One of the kittens looked a lot like Tiger, and she reached out to stroke its tiny head with one finger. Would Aunt Charity let her have it?

Then she had an idea. Megan was lonely these days, and a kitten might be just what she needed to fill the hours while she, Tabitha, and Abigail were with their tutor, or their "tootler," as Meggie said. She knew her aunt did not encourage pets, but perhaps she would see the advantage of having a cat around to catch mice when they came in from the fields, seeking a winter home in the Armstrong pantry. She could certainly point that out to her, anyway.

"I'll have to ask Aunt Charity," she said.

"Very well," Gabrielle said. "I am sure she will understand how badly you want it! Now, go quickly and complete our errand!" Gabrielle urged.

As she turned to leave the stoop, Sarah heard the door shut behind her and the latch slide into place. Was there reason for Gabrielle to be so afraid? She hurried down Waller Street and up Nicholson to the Palace Green, where the militiamen were drilling in the fading light. Of course, Hester had taken to locking the doors at night now, too, with all the strangers roaming around Williamsburg.

Quickly, Sarah slipped inside the palace gates, and made her way through the sculptured shrubbery. As she was passing the maze, a hand reached out, grabbed her wrist, and pulled her inside the dark, leafy tunnel. Before she could loose the scream in her throat, a hand covered her mouth.

"Do not scream, Sarah," he breathed in her ear. "It is Alistair." He removed his hand from her mouth.

"You nearly scared me to death!" she hissed. "Let me go!"

"Calm down, little American spitfire," he ordered, "or I shall be obliged to calm you down."

Sarah tried to glare at him, but she knew her efforts were wasted in the dark maze.

"That's better," he said, finally letting go of her wrist. "Now, you have something for me, my dear? Something from my cousin?"

She fumbled in her apron pocket and pulled out Gabrielle's note. "Here," she said, handing it to him. "Now show me the way out. I can't breathe in here!"

He took the paper and stuffed it inside his right stocking. Then he held aside a branch and motioned for her to go before him. Suddenly, just beside the entrance, he froze. Sarah, too, heard the footsteps, then voices.

"He surely would not come here, Governor," a man's voice said.

"He might, Tom. He's a bold one. And extremely clever. He would think, just as you said, that we would not expect him to come here, so what better place to hide? Especially in that infernal maze! I can't find my way through it in broad daylight!"

Sarah held her breath. Were they looking for Alistair? She turned toward him in panic, but he had vanished like a shadow, without a sound. What if they caught her here? Would they suspect her of contacting him, or would they assume she was just out for her usual walk in the lower gardens? And should she wait here in the maze, hoping they wouldn't find her, or should she step out boldly, as though she had no hidden purpose? Marcus had promised to speak to the governor for her.

Swallowing her terror, she was ready to take her chances on Marcus's influence with Governor Henry when he said,

★ Chapter Nine ★

"We will never find him in the dark, Tom. The man is like a shadow, gliding here and there through the night, never seen. But in a day or so, our armies will feel his evil influence in the knowledge the British have of our secret plans for some new offensive, of our hidden stores of supplies, of our strengths and weaknesses. The man is uncanny!"

"That's why he is known as the 'Demon Devon!' " the other answered. "I say he has help right here in Williamsburg, Governor. How else would he manage to elude our militia as he comes and goes so freely, gathering his deadly information? It seems the very walls have ears!"

"Or that our secrets are carried to him on the wind, an ill wind, indeed, Tom," the governor added.

The voices were moving away, and Sarah let out her breath. Were they referring to Alistair? Had she, after all, unwittingly aided a British spy in her desire to help her beloved tutor? And, if Alistair was the 'Demon Devon' the governor and his companion sought, did Gabrielle know? Surely she did not, for Sarah was convinced that her tutor and friend would not put her in the position of assisting the British against her own family.

She waited for what seemed like an eternity, then slipped out of the maze and through the ballroom gardens to the gates, and outside the palace grounds.

As she crossed the Green, she heard the gates clang shut behind her, and the lock turn. Then she began to run down Nicholson Street, to the safety of the Armstrong house.

As she went through the gate and into the house, she prayed her evening's adventure would not show in her eyes. She surely would have to face Aunt Charity's displeasure that she was arriving home after dark. As Hester Starkey had pointed out on several occasions, her aunt would have questions, and Sarah knew she had better have answers!

Perhaps she could distract her—as she had another day with the news that she had found a tutor—with the idea of a kitten for Meggie.

10

The days slid quickly toward autumn, and wild blue farewell-to-summers replaced the white daisies and golden black-eyed Susans along the lanes. The big oaks around town had not yet started to change color, but the maple leaves were showing a tinge of orange, and the crisp scent of the turning season was in the air as Sarah and her cousins made their daily trips to the tutor's.

Sarah had dreaded going back to Gabrielle's alone for her evening sessions after her meeting in the palace gardens with the Englishman. But once Gabrielle had been assured that the secret mission had been accomplished and Alistair had slipped away safely, she never mentioned it again. Sarah was greatly relieved.

Not that she lacked courage. She was, after all, as Gabrielle said, "the brave Kentuckian." She had been frightened, of course, when Alistair pulled her into the maze, and when they had nearly been discovered there by

Governor Henry and his companion. But it was not fear that prompted her dread of being asked to carry another message past the militiamen. It was that nagging doubt that, no matter what Gabrielle said, by aiding the Englishman, she would be harming the American cause so dear to her brother's and uncle's hearts.

As the weeks passed, though, and Sarah was not asked to undertake another such mission, she began to relax and enjoy again her evening sessions with Gabrielle. Surely Gabrielle was exactly what she seemed—a pleasant, interesting, well-read, well-traveled teacher, giving her pupils all she could to enlarge their narrow horizons. She was the kind of teacher Sarah vowed she would be someday.

A few weeks later, with Aunt Charity's blessing, Sarah carried the little striped kitten home to Megan, who, in response to Sarah's story about her own cat named Tiger, promptly named the kitten Tiger too. From then on it became almost impossible to get Meggie to come into the house, where the immaculate Aunt Charity would allow no cat to enter.

Then, overnight it seemed, the frost painted every tree in Williamsburg, and all but the hardiest flowers along the lanes and in the gardens turned brown and drooped on their stems. The wind in the Armstrongs' cedar tree murmured restlessly, warning of winter.

Sarah had less time to spend in the palace gardens now, with the days growing shorter and her evenings taken up by the extra Latin, history, and literature lessons, but she went whenever she could. There, amid the scent of dying vegetation, the evergreens were as green as ever, and purple ageratum and the small pink, white, and wine globes of amaranth still brightened the beds down by the maze.

Sometimes she saw Marcus, busy raking fallen leaves and removing dead flowers from the gardens. Once she saw him loading a wheelbarrow with broken bricks he had replaced in a wall. He always waved and called, "How you been, Miss Sarah? And all your folks? Have you all heard from the colonel?"

And she would reply that all was well with the Armstrong household, but, no, they had not heard from her uncle. They assumed he was all right.

In late September, Sarah slipped off alone one day after their afternoon lessons to buy some nonpareils with the last of Nate's coins. When she purchased the candy, the clerk at Greenhow's store handed her a travel-stained letter.

"It was left off here by a man who came to seek help for the Kentucky settlers. They say the Indians are being paid by the British to take their scalps!" he explained.

★ Stranger in Williamsburg ★

With shaking hands, Sarah pried off the sealing wax and opened the letter. It was dated "12th August," and in it, Ma wrote that they were all fine; they missed her terribly; and they all sent their love. She asked her to pass on regards to the Armstrongs from the Moores, and explained that she could not write more because the man who would carry the letter to Williamsburg was ready to leave. She had not known she would have this opportunity to send a letter until they had arrived at the fort that day, seeking protection from increased summer Indian raids.

Sarah felt tears sting her eyes as she refolded the letter. Ma's words had brought her so close! How she longed to see her, all of them! But, at least they were alive and well back in August.

A few days later, Sarah's Uncle Ethan came home, spent the night, and was gone before she and her cousins had arisen the next day. Aunt Charity said he had come into their rooms and stood watching them sleep for a few moments. He had asked her to give them all his love—"You, too, Sarah," she said—and to assure them that he would see them next time he was home, which, God willing, would not be too many weeks away.

Then, the broadsides posted in front of the Raleigh Tavern and Christiana Campbell's reported the heart-breaking news that 15,000 red-coated British soldiers had landed at Chesapeake Bay.

The redcoats occupied Philadelphia, and the Continental Congress fled to York, Pennsylvania. Shortly thereafter, General Washington's forces met defeat in the Battle of Germantown, but the Patriots won the second Battle of Freeman's Farm. Sarah prayed that Nate was safe.

Talk of the war was everywhere she went. Even walking

★ Chapter Ten ★

down Duke of Gloucester Street or shopping in Greenhow's store, Sarah overheard the stories. It seemed the British had knowledge of every plan the Patriots designed. They discovered stores of arms and supplies. They were prepared for every attack.

The rector of Bruton Parish Church even remarked one Sunday, "The British espionage system is very efficient and extremely well-informed. Governor Henry says our plans are carried to them on the wind!" He had paused to lean over the pulpit and glower down at the congregation. "But it is no wind that carries our secrets, my children," he said sternly, "and until we catch the spies among us, we cannot hope to win battles, much less this war!"

Then, one day in late October as they were returning from Gabrielle's, Sarah looked up to see a man walking up the Armstrongs' front walk.

Abigail gasped and grabbed Tabitha's arm. "Tabby, is that Pa?"

Tabitha narrowed her eyes to see better through the autumn haze. "Why, I believe it is, 'Gail!" she answered, and they ran to meet him.

Sarah was almost as glad to have her uncle home as his daughters were to see their father. The one time since she had been there that he had come home for a few days' rest and to get supplies, the house had been lively and happy, with even Aunt Charity in a happy mood. And there had been delicious desserts with every meal. It turned out that sour old Hester had a light touch with tempting sweets.

Now, as she came through the gate and saw Uncle Ethan gather his daughters to him in one big hug, Sarah was filled with longing for her own father, with his teasing Irish eyes and words.

93

"Where have you been this time, Pa?" she heard Abigail ask.

"Oh, here and about," Uncle Ethan answered evasively. "Good afternoon, Sarah," he said. "And how are you liking Williamsburg and the Armstrong household by now? Are you happy here, child?"

Sarah looked up into his kind, brown eyes, and saw real concern for her well-being. A rush of warmth spread through her. "I'm fine, Uncle Ethan," she answered. "And I'm glad you're home!"

"So am I!" he agreed, with a grin that stretched his generous mouth nearly from ear to ear. "So am I!"

"We have a new tutor, Pa!" Abigail interrupted excitedly. Then she and Tabitha both began to talk at once.

He held up both hands. "Whoa, there!" he ordered, laughing. "I don't want to hear anything about such serious things as tutors until I've stowed this knapsack in the study, freshened up a bit, and put away some of your ma's and grumpy old Hester's good cooking!"

He put an arm around each of his daughters and drew them toward the door, looking back to wink at Sarah. "I haven't had a really good meal since I left here. I do believe all they know how to cook up north is meat and potatoes, and always the same way!"

Sarah's feeling of loneliness grew all through supper as she listened to Abigail, Tabitha, and Megan chatter to their father of all they had been doing since they last saw him.

"The cat's got your tongue, Sarah!" Megan leaned over to whisper in Sarah's ear, as the two older girls vied for their father's attention.

"I can't get a word in edgeways, Megan!" she whispered back, attempting to hide her loneliness. She knew the

Armstrongs did not mean to exclude her. They were just excited to see their pa, as she would be to see hers, if she could.

"Me, neither!" Megan agreed. She sighed and went back to pushing squash and beans around on her plate.

Finally, Aunt Charity stood up and announced, "We will have our coffee and apple pie in the parlor, Hester. Girls, you may join us, since it is your father's first night home. Abigail, perhaps you could play one of your new pieces for us on the harpsichord."

Delighted at being the center of attention, Abigail sat down at the musical instrument and began to sort through sheet music.

Sarah watched as her aunt and uncle seated themselves side by side on one of the brocade love seats, and Tabitha dropped onto a stool in front of them. Little Megan crawled up into her father's lap and snuggled against him. Sarah saw Uncle Ethan take Aunt Charity's hand in one of his. Then he rested the other one on Tabitha's shoulder, and she looked back at them with a contented smile as Abigail began to play a lilting tune.

A pang of loneliness shot through Sarah. She pictured Ma bustling around the fireplace, while Pa played his dulcimer, and Luke sat whittling an animal that had little Jamie dancing around the room in his impatience to add it to his farm. She could almost see the flickering firelight playing over the dear faces, hear the tinkling sound of the plucked dulcimer strings, smell the pungent odor of cedar shavings. She blinked away tears.

Her uncle went over and threw open the back window. "I declare, Charity, it's only October and you've got such a fire going we could roast a goose in here!" He stood by the window, fanning himself with one of the draperies, as Hester served pieces of apple pie on small flowered plates.

"Now, ladies," he said, sitting back down with his pie and accepting from Aunt Charity a cup of fresh coffee laced with cream, "Let's hear about this new tutor of yours. Are you learning a lot?"

"Oh, Pa, she's the most beautiful woman I've ever seen!" Tabitha began. "And she serves tea so elegantly, and . . ."

"She smells so good, and she wears clothes made in the latest fashion from Paris, France!" Abigail interrupted.

"By the way, speaking of France, I hear that General Burgoyne's surrender at Saratoga has encouraged the French to come openly into the war, after all these months of supporting us in secret!" Uncle Ethan reported. "But back to your tutor. And I'm more interested in who she is and what she is teaching you, than I am in her clothes and perfume. Sarah, you haven't commented. What do you have to say about this wonder tutor?"

"Her name is Gabrielle Gordon," she began, "and she knows French and Latin, and she is very interested in you, Uncle Ethan."

Sarah saw the light in her uncle's eyes darken, as he looked quizzically at his wife. "Gabrielle Gordon, did you say?" he asked.

Sarah nodded, for some reason feeling a chill settle over her in spite of the stuffy warmth of the room.

"Miss Gordon runs a new millinery shop down on Waller Street, Ethan," Aunt Charity explained. "She seems intelligent, and very charming."

"I've no doubt she is!" he exclaimed. And, again, a chill struck Sarah. There was something alarming in her uncle's look and tone of voice. "I'd like to speak with you alone, my dear," he said gravely to Aunt Charity.

"Leave us, girls," Aunt Charity ordered immediately, a frown creasing her forehead and a troubled look in her blue eyes. "You may go to your rooms. We will see you in the morning."

Sarah felt her heart sink. Something was terribly wrong, and it obviously concerned Gabrielle!

11

Tabitha paused with one foot on the stairs and her hand on the bannister. "Coming up?" she asked. "We could play a game of . . ."

"We'll be up in a minute, Tabby," Abigail said loudly, "as soon as we get a drink of water."

When Tabitha turned and went on upstairs, Abigail placed one finger over her lips, grabbed Sarah's arm, and pulled her toward the kitchen and out the back door. She let go of her then, motioning for her to follow as she crept across the yard to sit under the open parlor window.

Sarah followed, uncomfortable with the idea of eavesdropping on Aunt Charity and Uncle Ethan's private conversation, but anxious to hear what her uncle had to say about Gabrielle.

". . . spends most of her evenings in Christiana Campbell's Tavern listening to the men talk about the Revolution," he was saying as Sarah dropped silently beside

Abigail. His words were as clear as though they were still in the room. "We've suspected her for a while, but she's very clever. We haven't been able to catch her passing on what she hears to her British contact, whoever it is. Most likely it's the infamous Demon Devon who eludes our every trap! If only I could get my hands on him!"

"But, Ethan, she's so gracious, so genteel, so . . ."

"So treacherous, Charity," he finished for her. "You heard Sarah say she's interested in me. I'm telling you, she only tutors our children to gain information about my activities and the action of the colonial army. She's a Tory, Charity, a Loyalist of the King of England! She has caused untold damage to our efforts, and she would see me hanged by the British in a heartbeat!"

Sarah gasped, inhaling the horsey scent of boxwood. She turned to find her own shock mirrored in Abigail's wide blue eyes. Her mind whirled dizzily. Surely Uncle Ethan was mistaken! Gabrielle couldn't be a spy!

It was true that she spent many evenings at the tavern next door, and what was it she had said the first time Sarah met her, about the English and French blood warring in her veins? Had the cool English blood of the Gordons won out, then? Were her seemingly innocent questions about the Armstrong household and its master not so innocent after all?

"But she hasn't been here long, Ethan. Can she have caused so much damage in so short a time?"

"Charity, someone here in Williamsburg knows every move we make before we hardly know we're going to make it! And, until recently, our leaders were able to discuss their plans at Christiana Campbell's or the Raleigh. Now, the British are waiting for us everywhere we go. They destroy or confiscate our supplies. They fortify in advance the places we plan to attack. They know where to intercept our marches."

No! Sarah thought. *It can't be true!* Gabrielle was her friend. Sometimes it seemed she was the only friend Sarah had here in Williamsburg. She simply could not be a British spy, seeking to harm Uncle Ethan! Then Sarah recalled Gabrielle's British cousin, and the accusations that he was a spy. What if her uncle's words were true?

Her thoughts flew to Nathan. Would Gabrielle hang him, too, with her pretty words and charming smile? Would she pass on secrets that would enable the British army to capture or kill her brother?

Suddenly, Sarah's heart contracted painfully. Who was the man she had met in the palace gardens? Was he Gabrielle's cousin, as she said, unwelcome now because he was British? Or was he the one to whom she passed on information about Patriot plans?

Sarah felt her face, then her body flush hotly. Had she aided the British cause by meeting this man in the gardens? And that list of supplies she had delivered to him? Were they something else besides an order for milliner's goods, after all? She had not seen the list. The sealed papers could have been anything!

Would Uncle Ethan consider her a spy, also, for the unwitting part she had played in Gabrielle's scheme? But it could not be true! It just couldn't!

Sarah felt Abigail's hand on her shoulder, pushing her back into the bushes, just as her uncle came over to stand by the open window.

"The gardens are still lovely, my dear," he said. "You've managed well in my absence. The cattle brought a good price, and the quality of the sheep's wool from the summer shearing was excellent." There was a silence, then he said, "I'm sorry you've had to do so much alone, but you know how important my work is. Once this war is over, I promise to make it up to you, God willing."

"Oh, Ethan," Sarah heard Aunt Charity say in a tearful voice she'd never heard her use before, "I'm so sorry for the mess I've made with the girls' tutor!"

"There's little harm done, Charity," he assured her. "We will simply tell Miss Gordon her services are no longer needed, and that will put an end to the whole affair. I just wish I could catch her at her unholy game!"

The voices moved away, and Abigail grabbed her arm. "We've got to get upstairs and into bed before they come to look in on us!" she hissed. "Hurry! Up the back stairs!"

Sarah sank back against the rough brick wall of the house. She knew her legs were too weak to hold her up, but she had to see Gabrielle. She had to know if what her uncle said was true.

"I've got to find out if it's true, Abigail!" she whispered.

"Of course, it's true, Sarah!" Abigail whispered back, indignantly. "Do you think Pa would lie?"

"No, I'm sure he wouldn't. But he could be mistaken."

"My father is never mistaken," Abigail insisted. "Even those times I wish otherwise."

"Well, then, maybe there's some explanation Gabrielle can give us. Please cover for me, 'Gail. I will be back in a few minutes," Sarah said. She looked back to see Abigail going in the back door as she ran around the house.

Nicholson Street was dark under a black sky without moon or stars. Sarah couldn't see anything at all. She wished for her cloak as she hurried down the street to where it joined Waller. The wind was chilly, and a fine mist of rain had begun to fall. In the distance, she could hear the tramp of boots as a military group marched in time.

Sarah knew Aunt Charity would have a conniption if she knew she was out here alone on this dark street, with soldiers—and spies?—all over town. But she had to see Gabrielle, question her. Warn her? If Gabrielle were being falsely accused, as she claimed her cousin had been, Sarah knew she had to help her somehow.

And if the accusations were not false? The suspicion burned its way into her mind. What would she do then?

Sarah arrived at the little brown house and knocked softly on the front door. When Gabrielle slid back the latch and let her in, Sarah saw at once that she was upset.

"My cousin is here again, Sarah, and it still is not safe for him to go about the streets of Williamsburg, with hot-blooded Patriots on every corner and in every place of business." She wiped the palms of her hands down her pale green skirt, and a wet spot appeared where each hand touched the silky material.

"What can I do, Gabrielle?" Sarah asked, her thoughts going back to Uncle Ethan and his accusations. She couldn't go to him for help. He was convinced Gabrielle was a spy.

"*Chérie*, all I need is a map to help Alistair find a way to slip past the militiamen and out of town. If he can get to the James River, there will be a boat to take him where he will be safe."

"A map?" Sarah repeated. "But I don't have a map, Gabrielle. I have never even seen one in the house."

"Your Uncle Ethan came home today, did he not? He will have one, *chérie*, in that little leather bag he carries."

Again, Sarah's thoughts went to her uncle's words about Gabrielle. "How do you know he came home? And how do you know he carries a map in his knapsack?" she asked suspiciously.

"Oh, all the soldiers do, *chérie*," Gabrielle said with a nervous laugh, ignoring Sarah's first question. "I am sure Colonel Armstrong is no exception."

"I can't ask Uncle Ethan for help, Gabrielle. You see, he . . ."

"*Chérie*, all I need is the map and the other papers your uncle carries in that bag. I cannot ask the Patriot Ethan Armstrong for help for my English cousin, whom they all believe is a spy, can I now? Will you get the papers for me, Sarah? You are my only hope!"

"Gabrielle! You want me to steal papers from my uncle?"

"Ah, *non, chérie!* Merely to borrow them for a very little while. Alistair is very bright, like you, Sarah. He can memorize the route out of here, and you can return the papers before your uncle ever knows they were gone."

Sarah's thoughts tumbled. She couldn't take her uncle's papers, even if it were only to borrow them, and even if he never knew! And, besides, she didn't really want to help the Englishman.

"*Chérie*," Gabrielle said, taking her by both arms and looking earnestly into her eyes. "My cousin's life depends upon it. Surely you would not condemn an innocent man to death!"

"Of course, not, Gabrielle! But I . . ."

"Please do this one thing for me, *chérie*, and I will never ask you such a favor again! Only this once. And I will be eternally in your debt!"

Sarah chewed her lip, her thoughts churning. She could

not take her uncle's papers! She could not aid an Englishman behind his back!

"Please, *cherie*," Gabrielle begged, sinking to her knees and holding up both hands in a pleading gesture. As Sarah watched in dismay, tears filled the beautiful dark eyes and spilled over onto the pink cheeks. "It is a matter of life and death, Sarah," she added. "It will not hurt your uncle. He need never know. Just slip the papers out, let us see them, and slip them back while he sleeps."

She reached out and clasped Sarah's hands in hers. "My own life will be in danger, *cherie*, if Alistair is found here in my house! Please, if you care for me at all, if our hours together have meant anything to you, save me now! You are the only one who can."

Sarah swallowed the fear rising in her throat. What harm could it do for them to see some old map? If she could get it without her uncle knowing. "I . . . I'll think about it, Gabrielle," she promised finally, unable to meet the gaze of the person she had grown to admire, to love above most others here in Williamsburg, and who now was asking such a hard thing of her.

Confused and troubled, Sarah turned and left the house, hearing the latch slide quickly into place behind her.

The night was as black as the inside of the maze, and Sarah's thoughts were just as dark. Could she do this thing that seemed so important to her friend, this "matter of life and death"? Should she? Was Gabrielle her friend, or was she, as Uncle Ethan believed, a British spy bent on destroying Sarah's own loved ones? What should she do?

If only she could talk it over with Ma or Pa! If only there were someone she could talk to, someone she could trust to advise her! But there was no one. Except Uncle

Ethan. She felt she could trust him, but he was convinced that Gabrielle was a spy.

Sarah still found that almost impossible to believe. They had been so close, shared such a delightful companionship. It had to be real! Gabrielle just could not be what her uncle believed! And Gabrielle wanted Sarah's help now. But could she do this awful thing?

It was raining harder now, and Sarah wished she could go back inside the house after her cloak. But she didn't dare. Not knowing anywhere else to go, she made her way to the Governor's Palace gates, but they were locked.

The wind was rising, blowing the cold, wet rain into her face as she turned to leave.

"Miss Sarah?"

At first, she thought she had heard her name on the wind, as she had when she was lost in the blizzard outside their cabin in Kentucky.

"Miss Sarah, is that you?"

Then she saw a lantern behind the iron gates, and recognized Marcus in its glow. "Yes, Marcus, it's me!" she answered, knowing now that she had hoped to find him here.

"What are you doing out so late on such a night, missy?" he scolded, unlocking the gates and drawing her inside.

"You almost missed me. If it hadn't been for a sick horse, I'd already be home eating supper! Come over here into the carriage house out of this weather and tell ole Marcus what's wrong."

He seated her on an upturned wooden tub between two carriages, and draped his own cloak over her shoulders. She pulled the heavy cloak around her, shivering. "Oh, Marcus, I don't know what to do!" she blurted out. "I need someone to talk to. I . . ."

"Well, honey, you go right ahead and talk, and if there's something he can do to help, ole Marcus will surely give it a try!" He sat on a small wooden keg across from her.

Suddenly Sarah didn't know what to say. She reached down to wring the water out of her soggy skirt and apron.

"You see, Marcus," she began finally, "I have this friend who means a lot to me. And she needs me to do something for her." She stopped again, not knowing how to tell him her problem without betraying Gabrielle.

He sat listening, waiting for her to continue, but she just sat there on the tub, wishing she had never come to Williamsburg, wishing . . . But, no, she did not regret coming here and meeting Gabrielle. She had learned so much from her. She had found such delight in her company. She just wished Alistair had never come to Williamsburg!

Marcus took out a knife and began trimming his fingernails. The moving blade reminded Sarah of Luke and his carving, and Luke reminded her of Ma and Pa, and the tears began to fall. Marcus handed her a clean blue handkerchief. She looked up at him. She had grown very fond of the old man, but she yearned for her own family now, as he must have longed for his all these years. Her loneliness ached inside her.

Sarah dabbed at her eyes with the handkerchief. "My friend needs . . ." she began. But how could she explain it all to him without telling him about Alistair, about her uncle's papers, about all the things that Gabrielle had asked her to keep secret?

"Friends are mighty important in this mixed-up ole world," Marcus said finally. "Even Almighty God gets lonesome for real, true friends. That's why He made Adam and Eve, I reckon. After He got through making the world and all the wonderful things He put in it, He just wanted somebody to appreciate it. Like when I work hard to make these gardens look pretty, I'm glad you're here to see them. If there's nobody to share what you do, Miss Sarah, it just doesn't seem so special."

Sarah wondered if he were thinking about his family and the lonely years he had spent without anybody to share his life.

"Most preachers don't talk about it that way," he said, "being so bound up in their 'Do unto others,' and their 'Give unto me's.' " He chuckled. "Even our rector here at Bruton Parish Church talks more about the war and our 'duty' to it, than he does our relationship with our Creator. He talks more about 'secrets on the wind,' than he does the Master of the wind."

Marcus sat there a moment, lost in thought, then he said, "If there are any secrets on the wind, Miss Sarah, I reckon they're secrets God's trying to whisper in our ears."

"What do you mean, Marcus?" she asked.

"Well, I heard this preacher once," he said. "It was during what they call 'The Great Awakening of 1740.' I was about thirty years old at the time, and ornery as they come!

But, somehow, my ma got me to this meeting. And I'd never heard anything like it! I've never been the same since that night."

"What happened?" Sarah asked, everything else forgotten.

"Well, I'd always thought our Creator was only concerned with 'mankind' in general, that we should just pray together in church about things like peace on earth and mercy for lost souls. But that preacher said God wants each one of us to be His personal friend, to hold a conversation with Him all day long, every day of our lives, just like I'm talking with you, here."

Sarah said nothing, her gaze fixed on the handkerchief she was twisting around her fingers. She had forgotten the damp chill of the unheated room, the beating of the rain on the carriage house roof, even why she had come here. Marcus talked about God just like her pa did, like he had just had breakfast with Him this morning!

Suddenly, Sarah realized the old man had stopped talking, and she had missed whatever he had said last. She looked up at him questioningly.

"The Son of Almighty God, Miss Sarah!" he breathed, his eyes glowing with the thought. "I just can't get over Him loving a no-account rascal like me that much! That preacher said if I was the only human being alive on this earth, Jesus would have died for me! That makes Him and me pretty special friends, I reckon."

He eyed her closely. "But I don't suppose your friend is asking you to do anything like that, is she?" he asked seriously, coming back to the topic at hand.

Sarah shook her head. "No, Marcus, but to help her, I would have to do something my family would not like." It sounded childish and unimportant after what Marcus had just told her.

"Families are mighty important, too, Miss Sarah," he said, as though he had read her thoughts. "Blood, they say, is thicker than water."

"But, Marcus, this wouldn't be likely to hurt my family in any way. At least I don't think so. It's just that they wouldn't understand what I need to do and why I need to do it."

Marcus pondered that a moment. "Will this deed you must do endanger you or anyone else in any way?"

She shook her head. "Oh, no. In fact, it could save a life, maybe two."

"One of them being your friend?" She caught a gleam of amusement in his dark eyes before he lowered them to study his newly trimmed fingernails. Did he think she was playing some childish game? She hadn't said her friend was an adult, but maybe it was better that way.

"Well, if it wouldn't hurt my family, and it would help someone else, then I guess I'd choose to help my friend," he said, getting up from the keg and dropping the knife into his pocket. He reached out a hand to help her up from the tub. "Now we'd better get you home before your aunt calls out the militia!" he said.

Sarah laughed shakily. "Oh, Marcus, that's all I need right now!"

Her gaze fell on the tub where she'd been sitting. Carved into its thick wooden bottom was a cedar tree with an eagle perched on its top branch. The design was exactly the same as the carving on her cup and the drawing in Uncle Ethan's study.

"What is it, Miss Sarah?" Marcus asked anxiously, noticing her fixed stare.

"That's what I want to know!" she answered. "It seems I run into that carving everywhere I go!" She pointed to the tub, then told him about the verses on Uncle Ethan's wall.

"Why, that's the mark of one of the Patriot groups working for the independence of the American colonies. Colonel Armstrong is one of its leaders. People who really believe in this Revolution carve or draw this and other symbols on their merchandise to show their support for the cause," he explained.

"But what does it mean, Marcus?"

"Well, it comes from the Bible. Ezekiel, I think. Or maybe Isaiah. And I reckon it originally referred to Israel. But the Patriots claim the eagle represents the spirit of freedom. They believe the Lord, Himself, will dry up and bring down the tall cedar—the old rotten government of England—and cause the branch 'planted by great waters'— the American colonies—to flourish," he added, as they left the palace grounds and walked down Nicholson Street.

At the Armstrong gate, Sarah handed Marcus his cloak and slipped quickly up the walk to the front door. When she looked back, all she could see was his lantern swinging in the darkness, turning north down Botetourt Street.

She tried the door, but it was locked! She hadn't even thought about not being able to get back in after Hester locked up for the night. Was there a chance the back door might be unlocked? Sarah ran around the house and pushed against the unyielding wood. Frantically, she looked around, and her gaze fell on the open parlor window. In their distress over Gabrielle, Uncle Ethan and Aunt Charity must have forgotten it.

Quickly, she climbed inside. She removed her wet shoes and stockings and carried them over to where the embers from the evening's fire still cast a faint warmth. She set her shoes on the hearth and hung her stockings over the fire screen. She held out her chilled hands, and then one foot at a time to the fire's fading glow.

Marcus's advice had been just what she needed, even if he had thought it was some childish game she played. He had said he would help a friend.

His words about Jesus came back to her. Marcus had said He was a special friend. Would He approve of what she was about to do? She didn't know. But if He understood about friendship, He would know how she felt about Gabrielle and why she wanted to help her.

Well, if I'm going to help my friend, she thought, forcing herself away from the welcome fire, *I'd better get it done, before I wake Uncle Ethan—or anybody else.*

She padded barefoot down the hall to her uncle's study, pushed the door open, and fumbled in the dark for the candle that always sat on the desk. She picked it up, and unable to find the tinderbox, carried it back to the parlor to light it from the fire. Then, shielding the feeble flame with her hand, she took the candle back to the study and set it on the desk.

Before her lay the stained leather bag Uncle Ethan had brought into the house earlier today. She threw a glance over her shoulder. The flickering candlelight sent shadows dancing around the room, and, for a moment, she thought she saw someone standing in the doorway. As she moved to close the door, she saw it was only another shadow.

Sarah's glance fell on the framed Scripture from Ezekiel. The candle that threw a warm pool of light over the desk, cast a deep shadow over the wall where the Scripture hung. She could not make out the words, but at least now she

knew what they were supposed to mean and why Uncle Ethan had them hanging there. Her little cup was more than just something to hold a drink, she thought proudly. It carried a symbol of the Revolution.

"Sarah, you are only procrastinating," she scolded herself silently. "You don't want to do what you know you have to do."

Quickly, her heart racing, she opened the pouch and removed the papers inside. She spread them over the desk. There was the map with all kinds of strange markings on it that were completely incomprehensible to her. The other papers seemed to be some kind of charts and lists, probably explaining the map she decided. She couldn't imagine why Gabrielle and her cousin wanted them, but Gabrielle had made it very clear that she should bring all of the papers.

Sarah folded them back into their original creases and

shoved them into her apron pocket. Then she replaced the pouch exactly where she had found it.

Sarah returned to the parlor and put on her wet stockings and shoes. She crept back down the hall and wrapped her cloak around her damp dress.

For a moment, she stood listening to the silence of the sleeping house, longing for the comfort of Abigail's deep, warm feather bed upstairs. Then, making sure the door was unlatched, she stepped out into the wet, dark night.

Ah, *chérie,* I knew you would not let me down!"
Gabrielle exclaimed, as she let Sarah into the shop. "I knew
you would help your Gabrielle. But it has been so long. We
were worried about you."

Sarah said nothing, watching the man in the parlor
doorway. He held out his hand. "The papers," he demanded.

Gabrielle threw him a look that made him drop the
hand to his side and step back into the room behind him.
She drew Sarah into the parlor and over to the fireplace.

"Give me your wet cloak and your shoes and stockings,
Sarah. I will hang them here by the fire to dry while Alistair
examines the papers." She stopped with the cloak in her
hand. "You did bring them, did you not, *chérie?*"

Sarah reached into her pocket and took out the papers.
She held them out to Gabrielle, but it was Alistair who
grabbed them from her and spread them out on the round
table under the lamp.

"Come, *chérie*. Sit by the fire, and I will fix some hot chocolate to warm your bones. What a miserable night it is, with the rain and the wind. I suppose the pretty leaves will be soggy piles beneath the trees by morning, and the flowers will be nothing more than a pleasant memory."

Still, Sarah said nothing. She was afraid that if she opened her mouth, she would be sick. Nothing about this seemed right. She sat by the fire, sipping the hot chocolate Gabrielle brought her, wishing she had never taken the papers, wishing she were home in bed and could wake up and realize it all had been just a bad dream.

From the corner of her eye, she could see Alistair feverishly copying something from one of Uncle Ethan's papers. She swallowed the sick feeling that rose in her throat.

"I've got to get back, Gabrielle," she finally managed to say. "I've got to get the papers back before . . ."

Gabrielle patted her hand. "He will soon be finished. Drink your chocolate. Then go into my bedroom, take off your wet dress, and wrap up in the warm robe you will find there. By the time you are ready to leave, your dress will be dry."

I am ready to leave now, Sarah thought miserably, but she did as Gabrielle asked. When she came back to the fire, wrapped in a warm, yellow robe, her dress and apron were hanging from the mantel.

"Before you know it, *chérie,* Alistair will be finished," Gabrielle assured her, "and you will have the papers back where they belong. Tomorrow, my cousin will be gone. You and your cousins can come for your lessons as usual, and you can forget this night ever happened."

She pulled a stool over near Sarah and dropped gracefully on it. "How is our Tiger kitten?" she asked. "Does

118

little Megan like him as much as you thought she would?"

"He's fine, and Meggie loves him," Sarah answered shortly. Gabrielle need not think she could be so easily distracted.

"I can see you are angry with me, *ma petite,* and I am sorry," she said then. "I certainly would not have asked you to come back out on such a night if it had not been extremely important."

Sarah stared at her in disbelief. Did she really think the problem with her being here was a little discomfort from the weather?

"Mademoiselle, it is not the weather that concerns me. It is . . ."

The tutor reached over and patted her hand again. "I know, *chérie,*" she said comfortingly. "I know. But there is no harm done. You will see. And your help means so much to Alistair and me."

Sarah leaned her head back against a wing of the chair. Fighting nausea and a drowsiness induced by warmth and her long day, she concentrated on the colors in the fire. Her thoughts went back to the night Luke had said they reminded him of Indian war paint. She wished all she had to fear around here were Indians! At least they had known where the danger lay out in the wilderness. Here, she did not know whom she could trust.

Was Gabrielle her best friend, or her worst enemy? Was she all she seemed, or was Uncle Ethan right? His words still rang in her head, "She would see me hanged by the British in a heartbeat!"

Would she? Sarah looked straight into the dark eyes, wanting to ask her point blank if the ugly accusations were true. Did she sit night after night in Christiana Campbell's or the Raleigh gathering information for the British, as Uncle Ethan said? Was Alistair her "kind and gentle" cousin, caught in a trap of unfair circumstances? Or was he the Demon Devon her uncle sought?

Sarah couldn't ask any of those questions, though, not with Alistair right here in the room with them. She pulled the robe more closely around her and tucked her bare feet up under it in the big chair. The next thing she knew, she awoke there, with one foot asleep under her. How long had she slept? The clock on the mantel said ten minutes until two o'clock—in the morning! The urgency of the situation returned to her.

I don't even know Alistair's last name! she thought suddenly. For all she knew, it might be Devon. He might be the Demon Devon the colonial army sought to capture and hang. Oh, she had to get those papers back and get out of here!

"Give me my dress, Gabrielle. I have to go, now!" she said.

To her surprise, Alistair stood up, folded the papers, and handed them to her. "Thank you very much, Miss Armstrong," he said with a smirk of a grin and a slight bow. "I am forever in your debt!"

"Moore," she muttered through clenched teeth. "Sarah Moore, not Armstrong!" But why did it matter? She had shamed both names beyond repair. *I probably should call myself 'Sarah Foolish' or 'Sarah Traitor,'* she thought, as she returned to the bedroom. She pulled on her dry, wrinkled clothes, and tucked the papers back into her apron pocket. The cloak was still damp, but she put it on, along with her shoes and stockings.

Gabrielle walked her to the door. "Not a word, *chérie*, to

★ Chapter Thirteen ★

anybody!" she cautioned. "And I will see you this afternoon."

Sarah hurried up Nicholson Street, wondering what might be hidden by the darkness all around her. If the Demon Devon was Alistair, she knew where he was. But if he wasn't, the British spy could be crouched behind that wall, waiting to pounce on her and take her uncle's papers. Or he might be lying in wait in the gardens behind that fence.

She heard a movement behind her and stopped to listen. But she could hear only the pounding of her own heart. She turned and peered into the darkness, but the blackness was complete. She couldn't even see the outlines of the houses along the street.

Turning to go on, she bumped into someone, and let out a small scream.

"Who goes there?" a voice cried, and she heard the rattle of a musket.

"It's Sarah Moore," she cried out, "Ethan Armstrong's niece." Her voice sounded as small and scared as she felt.

The militiaman peered closely into her face. "And what are you doing out at such an hour on a night like this?"

She recognized his voice. It was the young clerk who waited on her sometimes in John Greenhow's store. Her mind raced. What could she say? She could feel the papers burning a guilty hole in her pocket.

"I . . . I was at my tutor's, and I got sick and fell asleep by the fire. It was two o'clock before I knew it. If my aunt is awake, she will be frantic with worry. I must get home immediately!" So far, she thought in relief, she had not told a lie.

"Well, miss, we've posted sentries all around the town tonight. There's a notorious British spy on the loose. It's rumored he's in Williamsburg, so I'll just see you to your door. It wouldn't do for me to let anything happen to the niece of Colonel Armstrong, now would it?" He chuckled softly, and taking her by the upper arm, led her briskly down the street.

Colonel Armstrong would make sure "something happened" to me, if he knew what I've done, she thought miserably.

"Good night, miss," the sentry said at the gate. "And see you don't go gadding about Williamsburg in the middle of the night again. Leastways, not while this war's going on!"

"Good night!" she whispered, as she slipped inside the gate and up the walk. She could hear his quiet footsteps going back down Nicholson Street as she eased the front door open and went inside.

Hanging her cloak on a peg of the coatrack, she removed her shoes and stockings and set them in the brass tray under it. Then she padded on icy feet to the study. She opened the door, entered the room, and closed the door behind her.

Then she gasped, as a man arose from the chair behind the desk.

14

Sarah, where have you been?" Uncle Ethan demanded from the darkness. Her heart seemed to drop to her feet. "Do you realize that the infamous Demon Devon is creeping around Williamsburg tonight, and that he'd as soon kill a child as a soldier if she got in his way? Do you realize there is a war on and times are not as they once were?"

He fell silent as he lit the candle, and she searched her mind for answers to his unanswerable questions. She had not lied to the sentry, and she knew she could not lie to her uncle, no matter what the consequences. But what if her telling the truth would be responsible for Gabrielle's death? Could she endanger her friend?

Again, the thought came to her: What if his suspicions were right, and Gabrielle was not her friend after all? What if she really was a British spy who had used a trusting young admirer for her own evil purpose?

★ Stranger in Williamsburg ★

Outside, the rain lashed at the windows, and Sarah could hear the cedar tree moaning in anguish. In the distance, thunder growled, but the atmosphere here in the study was even more threatening as she faced the man who had been so good to her, and whom she felt she had wronged tonight.

"There are papers missing from my pouch, Sarah. Do you know anything about this?" His voice was hard, unyielding.

She met his stare for a moment, then dropped her gaze to the top of the desk where the empty pouch lay. Tears gathered in her eyes, and, again, she wiped them away.

She felt awful! He had been so kind to her, so caring. And now she had done this terrible thing, and there was no way around it. She might as well confess her crime and take her punishment.

Sarah reached into her apron pocket and drew out the papers. She held them out to him silently, flinching at the shock that crossed his face. His warm, brown eyes grew as cold and hard as Alistair's pale, blue ones. She could see his jaw quiver as he tried to control his anger.

He put both hands on the desk and leaned on them, as though he had suddenly become too weary to stand without support. "Why, Sarah?" She could see the pain in his face, and looked away, unable to bear it. "We have tried to be good to you, to offer you a home and every opportunity here in Williamsburg. And now you have betrayed my trust. Why, Sarah?" he asked again.

She stared at the desk, unable to meet his eyes, knowing he was right. She had betrayed his trust. It had seemed so right at the time! Even Marcus had encouraged her. Now it all seemed so ugly, so inexcusable. Tears welled up and spilled over. She couldn't stop them, so she let them fall.

There was no more use in trying to wipe them away than there was in trying to wipe out this horrible thing she had done.

"Well, we can get to the why later," her uncle said. "Sarah, I know these papers mean nothing to you, but they are very important to our cause, and they are vital to those who would oppose it. Who asked you to get them? Who has seen them?"

Still, she could not speak. Her gaze seemed glued to the offending pouch on the desk. Tears ran unheeded down her cheeks and dropped off her chin. She wanted to answer him, but she had no words.

He walked around the desk, took her by the arm, led her to a high-backed leather chair, and sat her down in it. Leaning over her, he said slowly and clearly, "Sarah, I have to know who has seen these papers. Many lives may depend upon it. I have to know what I need to do to counter the harm you have done."

Sarah covered her eyes with both hands and began to sob. "I . . . I thought I was saving lives!" she mumbled through her hands. "I thought their lives depended upon seeing some old map and papers they said you carried in that pouch. They said it wouldn't hurt you, that you need never know!"

"Thank God the storm woke me!" he said fervently. "Thank God that I came down here to study those plans, and found the papers missing! Maybe there's still time to repair some of the damage before it's too late!"

Sarah felt his hands removing hers from her eyes. "Look at me, Sarah!" he commanded. "Who told you all these things? You must tell me!" He shook her arms, emphasizing the urgency. "Don't you understand, Sarah, that my life and the lives of whole companies of soldiers depend upon your help now! Those papers contain the plans for our next offensive and information about our stores of arms and supplies."

Sarah jumped up and threw both arms around his waist, sobbing wildly. "Oh, Uncle Ethan, I am so sorry! I wouldn't hurt you for anything! I am so sorry!" she babbled.

He sighed. "I believe you are, child. But, if so, you must help me now. Who asked you to get the papers?"

"She said her cousin was in danger just because he is British, and . . ."

"We are all British, or were until a year ago," he said bitterly.

"She said all he needed was a look at the map you carried to plan his escape to the James River where a boat was waiting for him," Sarah went on, unable to stop the flow of words now that the dam had broken. "She said all he needed was a look at the map and the other papers with it, and he would be gone. Then I could return your papers, with no harm done and no one the wiser. She said her own life was in danger if Alistair were caught in her house. I'm so sorry, Uncle Ethan!" she repeated. "It seemed so right when she was pleading with me! Now, it seems so terribly wrong!"

"Alistair Devon," he almost whispered. "The Demon Devon. I knew he had to be the one! Sarah, the man is uncanny. He has slipped out of traps it seemed impossible for any human to elude. That's why he's known as a demon." He studied her intently. "And his contact is Gabrielle Gordon, or you would not have cooperated with them."

She nodded miserably. "I thought she was my friend,

Uncle Ethan, and I wanted to help her!" The tears spilled over again.

"She used your friendship, child, your blind adoration, to gain her own ends. She is as diabolical as her so-called 'cousin.' But we will discuss that later. Now there is no time to lose! I must try to stop Devon from escaping Williamsburg. I must keep those papers from getting into the hands of the British generals. I pray it is not too late, already. We have posted sentries all around town tonight, but he has eluded them before."

He left the room, then came back. "Sarah, do not leave this house until I return, no matter what. Do you understand me? Can I trust you now?"

She nodded. "I understand, Uncle Ethan. I will obey you." She ran to throw her arms around his waist again. "Oh, please be careful! He has such cold, pale eyes! I am afraid for you!"

Gently, he removed her arms. "I will be careful." He smiled grimly. "Thank you for the warning. Now, remember, stay here until I return. And if I am not back by morning, tell Charity what has happened." With that, he was gone. She heard the front door shut firmly behind him.

Sarah ran to the front window. It was raining harder, and the thunder seemed closer. In a flash of lightning, she briefly saw her uncle, wrapped in a dark cloak, headed down Nicholson Street. Then the night was dark again. She stared into the blackness, her tears flowing as freely as the rain that poured down as though it never intended to stop.

Out back, she could hear the cedar tree's frantic moaning and whispering, urging her to some action. "Oooh, rush! Ohhh, rush!" it seemed to say. But she had no idea what she could do now to help, and Uncle Ethan had ordered her not to leave.

"Please, God, protect Uncle Ethan," she prayed fervently. "I know I don't deserve Your help, but You know he is a good man. And if anything happens to him, it will be my fault!"

Sobs overtook her again. She flung herself down on the rug before the unlit hearth, letting the storm of remorse sweep over her, as the rainstorm swept over Williamsburg and the deadly game of hide-and-seek being played within it.

15

Sarah awoke cold and stiff on the rug before the unlit fireplace. Once she had emptied herself of tears, she must have fallen asleep.

She went to the window and looked out. A drizzling rain still fell, and the dark sky matched her feelings. Where was Uncle Ethan? Had he come back to the house while she slept?

She walked barefoot into the hallway. Her shoes and stockings still sat under the coatrack, but Uncle Ethan's cloak was missing. He had not returned. Was he still out hunting Demon Devon? Was he lying dead in some ditch or woods, where he had tried to stop the Englishman's escape? What would she do if she had to tell Aunt Charity—and Tabitha, Abigail, and Megan—that he was missing because of her foolish actions? What would she do if she had to bear the guilt of knowing she had caused her uncle's death?

Miserably, she crept up the stairs and into Abigail's room. She discarded her still damp and wrinkled clothing and slipped on her nightgown. She eased into bed beside Abigail, who slept deeply, her arms and legs in wild abandon over and under the covers.

Sarah felt her bones sink wearily into the soft feather bed, but her mind was too keyed up for sleep. Where was Uncle Ethan? Why didn't he come home?

Suddenly, a new thought struck her. What would they do with Gabrielle? Uncle Ethan had said they would hang Alistair Devon. Would they hang her, too?

Sarah swallowed hard. Her feelings about Gabrielle were so confused. She longed to go back to the time before Alistair had come to Williamsburg, when the patchwork hours of the long summer days had been stitched together with the sturdy, dependable thread of learning and conversation and sweet companionship.

Or so she had thought at the time. But the thread had been rotten all along, woven of lies and treachery. There was no patch that could mend the raveled, gaping hole that the last few hours had torn in her relationship with Gabrielle. She could never forgive her for betraying their friendship, for using her like a pawn in a deadly game of chess.

Sarah turned over on her stomach and buried her face in the pillow, but there were no tears left to fall. She had not slept again at all when, at about what should have been dawn if the sun had planned to shine that day, she heard the front door open and shut softly. Then she heard her uncle's weary tread on the stairs.

She wanted to jump out of bed and see with her own eyes that he was all right, to question him about the fate of Devon and Gabrielle. But she didn't dare. She pretended to

sleep as he stopped in the doorway. She supposed he wanted to see if she had obeyed his orders. Then she heard him move on down the hall and enter the room he shared with Aunt Charity.

Still unable to sleep, Sarah laid quietly beside Abigail until she heard Hester bustling around in the kitchen. She got up then, washed at the basin, and slipped into the old brown hand-me-down dress Abigail had given her. She tied on her Sunday apron, hoping Aunt Charity wouldn't notice. Her gray dress and everyday apron were beyond wearing until she had a chance to launder them.

Taking dry stockings from the drawer, she padded downstairs to put on the still damp shoes she had left in the tray under the coatrack.

Hester looked up with the smirk she used for a smile as Sarah entered the kitchen. Silently, she handed her a bowl of eggs to prepare for scrambling. Sarah took them, glad of something to occupy her hands, if not her mind.

Aunt Charity joined them, as Hester motioned for Sarah to pour the beaten egg and milk mixture into the hot iron skillet.

"Mr. Armstrong was up all night and will be sleeping this morning, Hester," her aunt said without explanation. She threw Sarah a long, hard look before she swept into the dining room. Sarah felt her heart stop, then start again. Aunt Charity knew! She had seen the angry knowledge in her eyes.

What can I do? she wondered desperately. She couldn't sit at the breakfast table with Aunt Charity, knowing how she must feel about her. She couldn't eat, anyway, with the huge lump in her throat. What if Uncle Ethan had been killed last night, and she had to face Aunt Charity this morning with the news that, because of Sarah's betrayal, she had no husband? What if Sarah had to tell her three cousins that, because of her blind trust in the wrong person, they had no father?

Sarah thought of losing her own father, and pain tightened her chest. How could she have been so stupid? If only she had never met Gabrielle! If only she had never come to Williamsburg!

Thank God, though, Uncle Ethan wasn't dead. He was upstairs sleeping. No thanks to her! But at least she didn't have to live with the guilt of knowing her actions had caused his death!

Hester was looking at her strangely. "Are you going to eat breakfast this morning, missy?" she asked sourly. "Or are you going to stand there in my way like a bump on a log?"

★ Chapter Fifteen ★

Sarah stared at her blankly, knowing she had to go into that dining room, take her place at that table, and play Aunt Charity's cool game of pretending nothing had happened until the rest of the family had eaten and they could be alone. She dreaded the moment when she knew Aunt Charity would attack her with a vengeful tongue.

Sarah walked to the doorway and looked into the room. Tabitha, Abigail, and Megan were all passing their plates to be filled, talking quietly, as Aunt Charity required when they were allowed to talk.

Aunt Charity sat at the end of the table, silently filling the plates. Her face was innocent of any expression at all. But when she raised her eyes to her niece standing in the doorway, Sarah saw in them such anger that, as Ma sometimes said, she felt like "a goose had walked over her grave."

How could she enter that room, sit at that table, and pretend nothing was wrong, while Aunt Charity's seething hatred swirled around her? How could she sit there with Tabitha and Abigail—and especially little Megan—aware that they would soon know she had chosen to help a British spy against their own father?

Sarah knew she simply could not do it. She turned abruptly and went back into the kitchen.

"Where are you going, missy?" Hester growled from over by the stove, where she had set up the ironing board and was preparing to iron one of Uncle Ethan's ruffled white shirts.

Sarah didn't answer. She ran down the hallway, grabbed her damp cloak, and ran out the front door and down the walk. Uncle Ethan had asked her to stay there until he returned, and she had not betrayed his trust this time. Now, she could not stay any longer.

Sarah pushed through the gate, then stopped uncertainly. Where could she go? She could not return to the little brown house, she thought as she began to walk down Nicholson Street. But by the time she reached Waller Street, she had decided she had to see Gabrielle one more time. She had to confront her with her betrayal. She didn't see how, but maybe, some way, Gabrielle could explain away the hurt.

Perhaps Alistair had made her do it. She remembered his cold, pale eyes, and was sure he was capable of anything, just as Uncle Ethan said. That must be it! Sarah thought, turning down Waller Street. He had threatened Gabrielle with her life, and she had acted out of fear for her own safety.

Sarah nearly ran up the walk to the milliner's shop and tried the blue door. It was locked, as it had been lately. She knocked, then knocked again. "Gabrielle!" she called softly. "Are you there?" But there was no answer. She walked around the house and peered in a window. There was no sign of life.

Sarah wished she had waited to ask Uncle Ethan what had happened last night. Had they caught Alistair? Had Gabrielle tried to escape with him and been caught? Or killed?

She pictured the beautiful French-English woman with her grace and charm, with her gracious praise that had made Sarah feel so special. "You are like the wild cat, I think," she had said, "and I am like the fox—wily, sly, cunning." Had her fox-like cunning run out? Had all the excitement and gaiety that surrounded her been snuffed out like a candle? Where was Gabrielle? Surely someone could tell her!

★ Chapter Fifteen ★

Sarah began to run, back up Waller and Nicholson, over to Duke of Gloucester. But the thin crowd that had braved the rain moved up and down the street, apparently unaware of Gabrielle's plight—whatever it was—unaware of Sarah's desperate need to know.

In front of Chowning's Tavern, she saw a woman wearing a pink silk dress. The hood of her cloak covered her head, but she walked with a quick, graceful step. Sarah ran, dodging people, sliding on the wet bricks. Then the woman turned, and Sarah's hopes died. It was not Gabrielle.

Betsy came out on the front stoop to shake out a duster. "Sarah!" she called. "I have something to tell you!"

Sarah's heart skipped a beat. She hurried over to the steps.

"Seth Coler is gone!" Betsy said breathlessly. "He just up and left his apprenticeship and disappeared. But I'd wager pounds to farthings he's gone to war! Just like I said he would!"

"Have you heard news of the milliner whose shop is down on Waller Street?" Sarah asked, dreading the answer. But Betsy shook her head.

"I hear they think she's a British spy," she said, "but I don't know what's happened to her. She usually spends her spare time at Christiana Campbell's or the Raleigh. Chowning's is too common for the likes of her!"

"Thank you, anyway," Sarah said wearily. "I . . . I'll see you at church."

Sarah plodded back up Duke of Gloucester to John Greenhow's store. *At least I can get in out of the rain a moment*, she thought wearily.

She felt the current of excitement the moment she entered the store. People were gathered in clusters, talking excitedly. Obviously, there was some news. Sarah moved close to one group, listening to their conversation while pretending to examine the tin flutes in the wooden bin in front of her.

"They caught him red-handed just west of the palace gardens," one man commented.

"I hear he had a copy of Colonel Armstrong's map in his stocking," another said.

"Aye, and a list of arms stockpiles in the other," a third added.

"It won't take a jury long to convict him!" the first man put in, chuckling.

"That it won't, and it'll be the hangman's noose for old Demon Devon!"

"And that too good for him! I say they should have . . ."

The men moved away toward the door, and Sarah edged next to a group of women who were over by the ribbons.

". . . knew she was no better than she ought to be, with them foreign airs and fancy clothes," said one.

"Well, let's see her flounce her silks and satins now!" another added smugly.

Sarah wondered guiltily what the women would say about her if they knew her part in it.

"It's a shame, though," one said sympathetically. "She was so pretty, and so lighthearted. Now she's locked up in that filthy place that's not fit for a pig, much less a cultured woman like her!"

"Well, she is a pig, or she wouldn't be passing secrets to the British!" the first woman answered. "I say the gaol is too good for her!"

They must be talking about Gabrielle! Sarah thought. She

threw down the ribbon she was holding and pushed her way through the crowd.

She caught a glimpse of the young clerk's startled expression as she ran out the door.

16

Sarah hurried down Nicholson Street to the public gaol. She and Tabitha and Abigail had passed the place every day as they went to Gabrielle's for their lessons. Now Gabrielle was supposedly locked inside. But after what she had done, didn't she deserve it?

After the third knock, the door opened a crack, and the gaoler stuck his head out. Sarah had seen Peter Pelham many times, playing the organ at Bruton Parish Church, but up close he looked every one of his fifty-some years, and his blotched, red face testified to the years of heavy drinking.

"What can I do for you, miss?" he asked, not unkindly.

"I'd like to see Gabrielle Gordon, please, Mr. Pelham," Sarah explained nervously. "She is here, isn't she?"

"Aye, I've got her, and that Demon Devon, too. It's a good thing I've got mostly British prisoners of war in the men's quarters now, or he'd be torn apart!" He peered at her closely. "What do you want with our lady spy?"

Sarah paused. She hadn't taken thought to prepare a reason for her visit. "She, uh, was our tutor, and I need to ask her a question," she said truthfully, though her question had nothing to do with the lessons she had had at the milliner's house.

He studied her. "Haven't I seen you at church with Colonel Armstrong's family?"

"Yes, Mr. Pelham, I'm Charity Armstrong's niece from Kentucky," she answered, wondering if Aunt Charity or Uncle Ethan would ever claim her again.

The gaoler nodded, and swung the door open. "I don't suppose it will do any harm, since she's the only prisoner in the women's room right now," he said. "Follow me."

Sarah followed him to a closed door, which he unlocked with one of the keys on a ring that hung from the waistband of his breeches. He motioned for her to enter.

"When you're ready to leave, just pound on the door," he told her.

Sarah went through the door and stood looking around the small, dark room. The walls were brick and oozed moisture. The floor was littered with straw. The window was barred.

She heard the door slam shut behind her and the key turn in the lock. She took a deep breath to relieve the smothery feeling she got from knowing she was shut away here inside the gaol. It didn't help, for the air was stale and rotten-smelling.

A slight movement in a back corner drew her attention to a figure huddled on a pile of straw, a thin blanket thrown around her shoulders.

"Gabrielle?" she queried. In the dimness, the coppery hair looked a dull brown, and her pink silk dress was limp and bedraggled. Sarah found it hard to believe that this pitiful creature was the elegant lady she and her cousins had so admired.

The woman turned to stare listlessly at her from dull, dark eyes. Then a small light of recognition came into them. "Sarah?" She rose stiffly, and came toward her, reaching out to embrace her.

Instinctively, Sarah took a step back from her.

"Ah, *chérie*, you have come!" she breathed. "Can you do anything to get me out of this filthy hole? Can you plead with your uncle to help me?"

Sarah stared at her in disbelief. Her horror at Gabrielle's changed appearance was replaced with anger. "How do you have the nerve?" she said sharply. "After what you caused me to do to him? How can you dare to ask?"

Gabrielle stared at her blankly, then a sad knowledge dawned in the dark eyes. She turned away. "You have a right to be angry, child," she admitted wearily, her shoulders drooping under the dirty blanket.

"Why, Gabrielle? Why did you use me that way? I thought you were my friend!"

"It was the only way, *chérie*," she answered, turning back to look at her, but keeping her distance. "We needed the information, and we had no other way to get it."

Sarah's last hope died. "We," she repeated. "You were a part of it all along, then? Alistair did not force you to help him? I suppose it was because of the blood you share as cousins?"

Gabrielle seemed about to agree, then she dropped her gaze to her hands as she twisted them together in front of her. Sarah stared at the broken nails and chipped polish.

"No, Sarah. We are no kin, Alistair and I. We have been

friends since the childhood summers I spent in England with my father's family. He lived on the next estate, and we played together whenever we got the chance. When we grew older, we fell in love. We had planned to make the marriage when this abominable war is over."

She held out her hands in a pleading gesture. "What has happened to him, Sarah? Have you heard? Please tell me he is not dead!"

Sarah shook her head. "No, Mademoiselle. He is, in fact, here in this gaol, in the room where men prisoners are kept."

Relief flooded Gabrielle's face. "He awaits the trial, I suppose." Then darkness settled over her features. "They will hang him, *chérie*. He does not have the chance of a snowball in July!"

For a moment Sarah shared Gabrielle's grief, then she hardened her heart. Alistair Devon deserved whatever the jury gave him. He was a terrible man! An enemy spy! But she had had such feelings for Gabrielle for so long, she could not help offering her some comfort. "Maybe they will send him back to England, instead," she said.

Gabrielle shook her head, studying her ravaged hands as though they belonged to someone else. "They will hang him," she repeated bleakly.

"What will they do with you?" Sarah asked, looking around the cold, damp cell with its straw pallet in the corner. She gasped as something moved in the straw, and black, beady eyes looked out at her.

Gabrielle followed her gaze. "It is just one of the rats, *chérie*. They have been coming in and out all night. They come to eat the rotten food I cannot eat, I suppose, but they seem to leave me alone."

Sarah shuddered, fighting nausea.

"Oh, I suppose one can get used to anything, Sarah, if one must," she said resignedly. "It is the filth and the dampness that I find so hard to bear," she added. "But, then, I have no choice, do I, *m'amie?*" She fell silent, then sighed. Gabrielle reached out to Sarah again, but thought better of it and dropped her hands to her sides.

"I am so sorry, Sarah, for what I did to you. I cannot say that given the same circumstances I would not do it again. I will lie to you no more. But regardless, I hope that someday you will find it in your heart to forgive me. I hope you will remember only the beautiful companionship we shared, and the fondness we had for each other."

"Gabrielle, I could forgive you almost anything except pretending to be my friend, only to use me! I can never forgive you that, Mademoiselle, if I live to be 200 years old!"

Sarah walked to the door and beat on it with her fists.

"But, *chérie,* I was your friend. I grew so fond of you!"

As the gaoler opened the door, Sarah glanced back to see Gabrielle slumped on the dirty straw, her hands covering her eyes. But again, she hardened her heart. Hadn't Gabrielle used that same trick of false tears last night to persuade her to aid them in their wicked plans?

Anger carried her into the hall behind Mr. Pelham, and out through the front door of the gaol. She didn't even care that it had stopped raining, and a weak sun was trying to break through the pewter clouds. Her spine stiff, she walked to the street, then stopped.

"What am I going to do?" she said aloud. She simply could not stay in the Armstrong house after her betrayal of Uncle Ethan last night. The fact that she had not meant to betray them did not cancel the awful consequences of what she had done.

Sarah supposed she'd have to find some way to get back to Kentucky. She knew she could not travel through the wilderness alone, especially with this war going on and with the British paying the Indians for every Patriot scalp they could take. At least that's what the clerk in John Greenhow's had said the day he handed her Ma's letter.

Not wanting to pass the Armstrong house, she turned left and walked toward Waller Street. She stopped for a moment in front of the little brown house, then woodenly moved on down the street to the Capitol. She cut across the Capitol grounds, and by taking a roundabout way, came out beside Peyton Randolph's house at the corner of Nicholson and North England, above her uncle's property. From there, it was only a few steps to the gates of the palace gardens.

Cold and miserable in body and spirit, Sarah made her way past the maze to the bank of the north end of the canal.

Marcus was nowhere in sight, but the swans glided serenely on the smooth water below her, as though the whole world had not suddenly been turned upside down. The fat geese waddled over to see if she had brought bread crumbs, and hissed indignantly when they found that she had not.

Gabrielle must be hungry, she thought. *And she must be cold in that damp, unheated room. I saw her shiver under the thin blanket.*

Her thoughts went back to the cozy teas she and her tutor had shared. Then she recalled her last visit to the millinery shop, when Gabrielle had given her the warm yellow robe to wear and hot chocolate to sip while her clothes dried by the fire.

"I don't care!" she said aloud. "She buttered me up like a piece of bread for one of her teas! And all to persuade me to believe that what I did for her and Alistair was right. Nothing is too bad for her and her fellow spy!"

Sarah knew, though, that it wasn't the spying that upset her so. It was the betrayal of her trust that twisted inside her like a knife. And not only had Gabrielle betrayed their friendship, she had caused Sarah to betray her own family.

"How could I have been so stupid!" she said aloud. "How could I have let her talk me into taking Uncle Ethan's papers?"

Again, the knife twisted, this time wielded by guilt and shame. There was no way that she could make up for what she had done, no way to pay for her awful sin against her family. There was no way to get rid of this terrible guilt. But how could she live with it?

Suddenly, she could bear it no longer, and she threw herself on the damp ground, clutching her stomach where the guilt seemed to lodge, sobbing uncontrollably.

17

"Mercy me, Miss Sarah! What is it? Are you hurt?" Marcus cried. He threw down a basket of apples he was gathering and ran to her.

Unable to stop sobbing, she could not answer him.

He took her by the arms and tried to raise her from the ground. "Miss Sarah, are you hurt?" he repeated. "What happened?"

His obvious concern only made her cry harder. Finally, when she had cried until there were no more tears, she sat up and wiped her face on the hem of her apron. "Oh, Marcus, I'm not hurt," she managed to say, "at least, I'm not injured in body." Her voice caught on a dry sob. "But my heart is broken!"

"Miss Sarah, what has happened?" he asked again. "Maybe ole Marcus can fix it. You know what I told you that first day, here in these gardens. I'll sure be trying!"

She shook her head sadly. "I wish you could fix it,

Marcus. Oh, how I wish you could! But there's nothing anybody can do now. It's all broken into pieces, like a smashed egg, and nobody can put it back together again."

"Well, missy, there's few broken things that the glue of love can't fix," he said soothingly. "Why don't you tell me what's wrong, and let me judge whether it's hopeless or not?"

She looked up into the kind, dark face. Suddenly, the words came out, haltingly at first, then in a stream of hurt and self-blame that seemed to have no end.

"Oh, Miss Sarah, I'm so sorry!" Marcus said, when she finally ran out of words and breath to utter them. "I encouraged you to help your friend, but I had no idea it was something like this! I thought it was some game you were caught up in between one of your young friends and your cousins. I'm so sorry I didn't give you better advice when I had the chance!"

She shook her head. "It's not your fault, Marcus. You only encouraged me to do what I wanted to do, anyway. I really believed Gabrielle—that I was saving their lives, and that it wouldn't hurt Uncle Ethan or anybody else. I let her play me like Abigail plays the harpsichord!" She fell silent, too numb, too exhausted to reason it out anymore.

Marcus sat by her silently for a while in easy companionship. She could hear the crickets and cicadas tuning up for a concert in the wet grass. Below her, the swans sailed majestically along the canal. And somewhere over by the icehouse, a rain crow called. *Hasn't he had enough rain?* she wondered idly.

Beside her, Marcus stirred and changed position. He plucked a blade of grass and wove it through his fingers.

"What you need to do now, Miss Sarah, to my way of thinking," he said, "is forgive Miss Gabrielle so you can go ask forgiveness from Colonel Armstrong. Then just put it all behind you, and get on with living."

"Forgive Gabrielle?" she asked in disbelief. "I could never forgive her! She betrayed our friendship. Don't you understand, Marcus? She used me like a . . . a pair of scissors, or a . . . a dressmaker's form. She fit her evil plans around me and basted me right up inside. And now I can't get out of this tangled mess no matter what I do."

"Well, the Bible says we have to forgive to be forgiven, Miss Sarah," he said gravely. "The Lord Jesus, in the prayer He taught His disciples, said, 'Forgive us our debts as we forgive our debtors.' "

Sarah heard Marcus, but she had no intention of forgiving Gabrielle, so she said nothing.

149

"Now, there's no doubt in my mind, missy, that you've been wronged." He shifted position again, discarded the shredded blade of grass, and carefully selected another one. "But you've done some wronging, too, even if you did it innocently."

"I told Uncle Ethan I was sorry," she muttered.

"And did he forgive you?"

"I don't know. He was in such a hurry to go after the Demon Devon. He didn't seem quite so angry as he was at first, though."

"And what about your aunt? Did she forgive you? You've wronged the whole family, you know, even the whole Patriot cause."

Sarah stared at him, recalling the cold anger in her aunt's eyes at the breakfast table before she had run from the room. "Aunt Charity will never forgive me, Marcus. She hates me!"

"You can't control what your aunt does, Miss Sarah. Or your uncle, for that matter, though I'd venture to guess that Colonel Armstrong will grant you his pardon. He's known as a compassionate and understanding man. But all God requires of you is that you go to them, confess your guilt, and ask for their forgiveness. First, though, you must forgive the ones who have wronged you."

Sarah stared at him rebelliously, then, surrendering to his steady gaze, she looked down at her hands. "I don't want to forgive her, Marcus," she admitted. "I want her to hurt, like I do."

He patted her on the shoulder. "Of course, you do, honey. That's human nature. We want to pay back pain with pain. But the Good Book says, ' "Vengeance is mine; I will repay," saith the Lord.' All we have to do—and sometimes it's very hard—is truly forgive and trust God to work things out in His own way. I've found, more times than not, that people most always reap what they sow, and, thereby, get a chance to regret and repent."

She looked up at him doubtfully. "Have you forgiven, Marcus?"

"Have I forgiven what, Miss Sarah?" She could tell by the puzzled look in his dark eyes that he really had no idea what she meant. He had forgotten! She could never forget what Gabrielle had done to her!

"Have you forgiven what people did to you—putting you in the stocks just because they thought you were 'uppity'?"

"Oh, that!" He dismissed the stocks with a wave of one hand. "After the king's governor and his household fled back to England, some folks around here thought I was a Tory, just because I had worked for them, belonged to them until the governor's lady gave me my papers. But ole Marcus has found it best just to do his work, keep his nose clean, and not meddle in politics!" He chuckled.

"Sometimes I remember it," he said then, "but I don't dwell on it. The Lord Jesus forgave the people who nailed Him to that cross, Miss Sarah, and He hadn't done anything wrong. Ole Marcus has done some regrettable things in his time, honey."

"And have you forgiven the man who sold your family?" she blurted cruelly, then regretted her question as she saw him flinch with pain.

"Well, I haven't forgotten it," he answered slowly, staring off over the canal. He cleared his throat, then went on. "But when I remember and bitter thoughts come, I just start to pray for his immortal soul, and pretty soon I'm at peace again."

He sat there lost in thought for a moment, then he said, "Anyway, I've never had anything done to me like what the Lord Jesus had to suffer, Miss Sarah, and neither have you. And, yet, He just went right on loving them, about like a mother loves her child, no matter what."

"You talk like you know Him personally, Marcus. You sound just like my pa."

"When a man gives his life for you, Miss Sarah, you have to feel something special for that man," he said thoughtfully. "And when the Son of God Himself leaves the throne of glory and lays Himself down on this old dirt just like a bridge for you to walk on back to God, you have to open yourself up to a special relationship with Him."

He sighed, patted her on the shoulder again, and stood up. "Once you really understand how much He loves you, Miss Sarah, the things other people do to you don't seem to matter very much. At least not once they're over."

"But, Marcus, He can't love me. I've done such terrible things!" she almost whispered.

"The Good Book says, 'He that cometh to me I will in no wise cast out.' There's nothing there that says, 'Everybody except Miss Sarah Moore, who has done such terrible things!' "

She laughed with him, a little shakily.

"That invitation even has my name on it, and only God and I know what a pitiful person ole Marcus has been! The Lord Jesus has paid the price for our sins, Miss Sarah, past, present, and future. Once we accept that payment in our stead, all we have to do is ask, and the good Lord forgives us. And I've got a feeling that's all you'll have to do with Colonel Armstrong. But, remember, it all hinges on you forgiving Miss Gabrielle and the little things she did to you."

"Little?" Sarah echoed. "You call what Gabrielle did to me little? The woman has ruined my life! Because of her, I have done terrible things. My family hates me. I can't stay here. Which means I can't get an education and become a teacher. I will just have to crawl back to Kentucky like a whipped dog, and live like an ignorant backwoodsman for the rest of my life! And you call that little?"

She glared at him, but he give her a sassy grin. "It's not much compared to being nailed to a cross," he said.

"Oh, Marcus, you're impossible!" Sarah jumped up from the ground, brushing at her bedraggled clothes. "Yes, I will go to Uncle Ethan and Aunt Charity—and Tabitha and Abigail and Megan, and even old Hester Starkey—and humbly beg their forgiveness," she said then. "I know I have wronged them. I owe them that much. I could even forgive Alistair Devon, for I never invested any love in him in the first place. But don't ask me to forgive Gabrielle Gordon, Marcus, because I simply cannot do it!"

"Honey, ole Marcus is not asking you to do anything. It's the Lord Jesus who's asking. And I think, just like ole Marcus was once, you're going to be mighty miserable till you get things straightened out with Him."

"Meddling old man!" she muttered under her breath as she gathered her damp cloak around her and stalked toward the gates.

Again, her anger carried her out of the gardens, down Nicholson Street, and to the Armstrongs' front gate.

Sarah stopped and looked up at the brick house before her. Inside were all the people she had wronged in her blind love for Gabrielle. Well, not all, she thought honestly. If Uncle Ethan had not caught Alistair, many Patriot lives might have been endangered. Perhaps even Nathan, wherever he was!

Guilt settled over her, as heavy and uncomfortable as the soggy cloak around her shoulders. She trudged down the walk, dreading the confrontation ahead.

They were all seated at the dining table, just as she had left them at breakfast, except that Uncle Ethan had taken his place at the head of the table now for the noon meal.

Aunt Charity looked up as Sarah entered the room. Her blue eyes turned cold, and her mouth set in a thin, hard line.

Tabitha kept her eyes lowered, looking at her plate as she moved her fork aimlessly over her food.

Abigail threw her a spiteful look, then went on buttering a piece of Sally Lund bread.

Megan looked up and saw her. Sarah noticed that her eyes were red, as though she had been crying. She pushed back her chair, and ran to throw her arms around Sarah's waist. "Oh, Sarah, I thought you were never coming back! I thought you had gone back to Kentucky, for sure! And I . . ."

"Sit down, Megan," Uncle Ethan ordered. "She's here. Now, stop crying and eat your stew. Sarah, come have something to eat," he said kindly, motioning toward her customary place at the table.

Sarah stared at the plate that had been set for her beside Megan, just as though nothing had happened. The flowers on her ma's china were exactly the color of her pa's Irish blue eyes, and her longing to be back in Kentucky with people who loved her, no matter what, completely enveloped her.

"I'll tell Hester to bring another bowl of stew," Tabitha offered, getting up to go to the kitchen.

Megan smiled at Sarah. "I love you!" she mouthed silently.

Their kindness was too much for Sarah. "I'm so sorry!" she blurted through a new flood of tears. "I did not mean to hurt any of you, but I know now that I did a terrible thing. And I ask all of you to forgive me. Especially you, Uncle Ethan!" She knelt at his feet and looked up into his face, but her tears blurred his expression and made it impossible to know his reaction to her words.

"I will go back to Kentucky, of course," she went on, "as soon as it can be arranged. I hate to ask, Uncle Ethan, but can you help me? If there's not enough of Pa's money left to hire someone to take me, I . . . I'll get a job at one of the taverns until I have enough. I can even stay there, if you don't want me here until then."

"Don't be ridiculous, Sarah!" Aunt Charity broke in indignantly. "The very idea! My own sister's child working in a tavern!" She shuddered. "Of course, I will require you to write Della and Hiram and tell them just what their little girl has been up to lately!"

★ Chapter Eighteen ★

Sarah dropped her gaze from her aunt's eyes, wishing again that she were back in Kentucky where she could explain, face-to-face, to Ma and Pa. She felt sure they would understand, though she knew they would not approve of what she had done. But there would be love and understanding in their eyes, instead of coldness.

"Now, go change those awful clothes!" Aunt Charity continued. "I certainly hope no one saw you in the street looking like that!"

Her uncle reached down and squeezed her hand. "It's all right, Sarah," he assured her. "Your remorse is evident. You are forgiven. The Demon Devon is caught, with his copies of my papers still on him, and all is well that ends well. Go quickly now, and freshen up. Then come have something to eat." He smiled down at her, and she felt her chest fill with grateful warmth.

Sarah wiped her eyes with the hem of her muddy apron, and stood up. She looked at each of them in turn. Megan beamed at her. Tabitha smiled kindly as she came back to her seat.

"Sarah, would you please end this melodrama and let us eat before the stew is cold beyond bearing?" Abigail said crossly. "And there's blackberry pie waiting in the kitchen!"

Without another word, Sarah turned and obeyed. When she came back, wearing the only clean thing she had, her blue Sunday dress, she was grateful to find that the meal went on as though nothing had happened.

As Hester carried in the pie, though, Sarah's thoughts again went to Gabrielle's statement about the rats coming to eat the rotten food the prisoners could not swallow.

She recalled the French pastries the milliner had served

her pupils as a special treat, the special teas and breads they had sampled.

"I saw Gabrielle," she said, playing with her fork, unable to swallow the bite of pie she had on it. She looked up and found all their eyes upon her. "She's in gaol. Mr. Pelham let me talk with her a few minutes."

Uncle Ethan's brown eyes narrowed. "And has our little spy had time to repent?" he asked. Sarah was surprised to find no sympathy in his expression.

"I don't know about that. She's cold, though, in that damp, foul-smelling place. She had a thin, dirty blanket around her. I don't think she's had any food." Sarah shuddered. "There were rats in her cell."

"Oh, Sarah!" Tabitha breathed. Abigail, for once, was silent, a look of horror on her face, and Megan threw both hands over her mouth, her eyes wide with shock.

Aunt Charity arose from her chair. "Ethan, you know that gaol is no fit place for a woman, no matter how vile she may be. Can't you do something?"

He looked around the table at all their faces. Megan began to cry again. Finally, he crumpled his napkin and threw it on the table. "I'll see what I can do," he promised wearily, pushing back his chair and standing up.

"Wait!" Aunt Charity said. "I'll have Hester fix her a basket of food and find a warm cover for her." She headed briskly for the kitchen.

"I have a shawl she can have," Tabitha offered. "I'll get it."

"I could send her my . . . my new kitten!" Megan put in. Then tears welled again as she thought of giving up her pet.

"That won't be necessary, Megan," Uncle Ethan said.

"Mr. Pelham would not let her bring a pet into the gaol, I am sure."

Sarah sat there with mixed emotions. She still was angry with Gabrielle, and hurt by her actions. She hadn't meant to help her. The words had just tumbled out, from some well of compassion fed by happier times. Truthfully, though, she didn't want Gabrielle to be cold and hungry. She would do the same for her as she would for any stray dog. But her sympathy stopped there, she told herself. She could never give Gabrielle what she had begged of her—forgiveness.

Marcus's words echoed through her mind. "It's not much compared to being nailed to a cross."

"Leave me alone, Marcus!" she muttered, grabbing her plate with its uneaten pie and carrying it to the kitchen. "I will not forgive her! I have seen to it that she will be fed and have warm cover, and that's more than she deserves!" Furiously, she began to wash the tub full of dirty dishes, while Hester stared at her in amazement.

The afternoon stretched on and seemed to be the longest she had ever spent. She tried to read, but the book was one Gabrielle had assigned, and she could not concentrate on it. Gabrielle kept intruding.

The sun had given up trying to break through the gray clouds, and another miserable drizzling rain had begun to fall. Sarah could hear Abigail in the parlor practicing her music and found herself drawn to it.

Tabitha was seated on the stool in front of the fireplace. She looked up with a sympathetic smile. "Come help me cut out pieces for my quilt, Sarah," she invited, holding up a piece of the blue material from Sarah's Sunday dress and a pair of scissors. "I have some material from each of our new dresses, and some from one of Ma's old ones," she chattered on, as Sarah sat on the love seat and took the pattern and material she handed her.

Suddenly, Sarah remembered what Betsy had told her about Seth. "I have to tell you something, Tabitha," she said reluctantly.

Tabitha looked up eagerly, then her face paled and her hands grew still. "It's Seth, isn't it?" she whispered.

Sarah nodded. "Betsy says he left Chowning's. They don't know where he's gone."

Tabitha looked down at the quilt piece in her hand. "He's gone to war," she said quietly. "I think I knew before you told me. I've had this uneasy feeling in the pit of my stomach. He hasn't been out to slop the pigs lately."

Sarah wanted to comfort Tabitha, but "He'll be back," was all she could think of to say.

Tabitha nodded, her face bleak. "Help me pray for him, Sarah," she begged. Then she went back to her quilt making, as though it were the only thing she could do for her missing loved one.

Sarah cut pieces for her until, just as the clock on the mantel struck four, she heard the front door open. She stopped cutting, with the scissors in one hand and the material in the other, and listened to the heavy footsteps coming down the hall.

Sarah glanced at Tabitha, but she continued to work on her quilt. Abigail, though, had stopped playing the harpsichord, and sat watching the doorway.

"Well, your tutor is out of gaol," Uncle Ethan said. He strode to the fireplace and leaned wearily against the mantel.

Sarah heard Tabitha's sigh of relief, though she never

looked up from her quilt. Abigail picked up her tune where she had left it.

"Where is she, Uncle Ethan?" Sarah asked hesitantly.

"Only God knows!" he answered gruffly. "And I don't care, so long as she's far away from here! By now she should be well on her way to Norfolk, with a healthy contingent of militiamen to make sure she catches the next ship back to France."

Sarah felt her heart drop like a stone. Gabrielle was gone! She would never see her again!

She looked at each of their faces. Tabitha was intent on her stitching. Abigail played her merry tune, keeping time with the swaying of her head. Uncle Ethan stared into the fire. None of them showed a hint of concern for the former tutor, turned spy.

"You must forgive to be forgiven, Miss Sarah," Marcus had said. She had been forgiven, though, by her uncle and his family, and, she supposed, by God. But Gabrielle was on her way out of the country, with the heavy burden of Sarah's judgment upon her.

Sarah's heart ached. Their relationship had been so special. Gabrielle had taught Tabitha and Abigail what they wanted to know, what Aunt Charity wanted them to know. But for her, she had opened a window on the world that Sarah knew could never be shut again as long as she lived.

With words, Gabrielle had taken her to London, to Paris and Rome, to Boston and Philadelphia. She had shown her the gardens of Versailles, the changing of the guard at Buckingham Palace, the art treasures of the Louvre. She had ridden the canals of Venice, and explored the rich vineyards and country estates of Bordeaux. Never again would she be the same ignorant, country girl who had stood on Duke of Gloucester Street last May and thought it the most exciting place in the world.

Thanks to Gabrielle, she thought sadly.

Suddenly, Sarah knew she had to see Gabrielle again, just once more before the opportunity was lost to her forever.

Sarah stood in front of the brown house, hoping against hope that the blue door would swing open, and Gabrielle would appear. She pictured her standing on the stoop with her luggage around her, getting into a carriage, turning to look at her out of sorrowful eyes, and raising one hand in a graceful farewell as the carriage pulled away.

Sarah recalled the easy companionship of the hours she had spent with the beautiful French-English lady—listening, learning, laughing, as Gabrielle became her dearest friend.

"You and I are cut from the same cloth, *chérie*," she had said once, as she cut a fashionable new dress from a golden silk brocade. Sarah had looked up questioningly from her translations, and Gabrielle had laughed, that warm, bubbling laugh that always sent ripples of excitement through her. "We share the cat's intelligence, curiosity, and love of adventure, *chérie*. But, alas, we also share the hardheadedness, the stubbornness, the determination to do things our own way."

She had laughed again, and reached out to brush the hair back from Sarah's eyes. "Be careful, little kitten," she had warned, "or you will use up your nine lives early, as I suspect I am sure to do."

Sarah could almost see her standing there on the stoop of the little house where they had spent so many happy hours together. But, of course, her beautiful tutor did not appear, and, sadly, Sarah walked on down Waller Street toward the Capitol.

Had Gabrielle used up her nine lives? Or would she go back to England, or to France, and make a new life there? Would she tutor some other young girl, open for her that window on the world she had led Sarah to look through?

Suddenly, Sarah knew that it did not matter what Gabrielle had done. Like Marcus and the slave trader, she supposed she would never forget. But nothing could cancel out the exciting things she had taught her, the joy of learning and adventure she had given her. They would continue for the rest of her life.

"I have to see her!" she choked. "I have to tell her that!"

Sarah crossed the Capitol grounds to Duke of Gloucester Street and wandered its length, unaware of the merchandise that beckoned from the shop windows or of the unconcerned crowd that jostled her.

"I have to see her!" she repeated. But Uncle Ethan had said that Gabrielle was well on her way to Norfolk. If only she could overtake her, talk to her just for a moment! But how?

"If ever you need a friend, all you have to do is yell." The words echoed through her memory. Marcus! She would find Marcus and ask him to take her to Norfolk.

★ Chapter Nineteen ★

She hurried to the palace grounds, but the gates were locked, and Marcus was nowhere to be seen. Had he gone home for supper? Where was his home? She recalled watching him walk away from her the night he had encouraged her to help her friend. He had gone north at Botetourt Street, but where he had gone from there, she had no idea.

Abigail had told her that many of the freed slaves of Williamsburg had cottages on the outskirts of town in a place known as "Raccoon's Chase."

Sarah took the back alley to Botetourt, then headed north across the fields in the Chase's general direction. Soon she came to a row of small wooden houses along a muddy path. Was one of them Marcus's? If so, which one? Sarah carefully made her way down the path, stepping on stones and an occasional tuft of weeds to keep out of the mud. She smelled wood smoke mingled with the rancid odor of old bacon grease and wrinkled her nose.

Then she knew which house was his. It had to be the one with the marigolds and asters abloom along a walk made of broken bricks. The walk led to a very small house with a deep red front door. The flowers were the same kinds as those in the park below the palace gardens that Marcus tended with such care, and the bricks were the same color as some in a pile she had seen in the gardens.

At her knock, Marcus came to the door with a big wooden spoon in one hand. He had a white dish towel tied around his waist. "Why, Miss Sarah!" he gasped. "What's wrong?"

All at once, the words just tumbled out. "Oh, Marcus, she's gone, and I've just got to see her once more! I didn't get a chance to forgive her, like you said I must do! And I know now that I really need to do that, Marcus. I need to tell her . . ."

"Hey, slow down, missy!" he begged. "Who's gone? Your tutor? And where has she gone? Do you know?"

She nodded miserably, swallowing the tears that threatened again. How could there be any more tears, she wondered, after all she had shed? "They're taking her to Norfolk to catch the next ship to France."

"They've released her from gaol? Then, honey, she's blessed to be going home! I was sure they'd hang her!"

"But, Marcus, if I could just follow her to Norfolk! Surely the ship won't sail as soon as she gets there. And I could talk with her, tell her I have forgiven her. It was important to her, Marcus! She begged me to remember the good times we shared. And we did share so many! But I told her I'd never forgive her if I lived to be 200 years old!"

Why was he staring at her that way? She paused for breath, but the words would not be stopped. "And now she's gone, and I don't know how to reach her in France, and she'll spend the rest of her life thinking I hate her. But I don't. She wronged me, but, before that, she gave me so much, Marcus! I've just got to tell her! And you promised . . ."

"All right, Miss Sarah!" he laughed, raising his hands in surrender, the wooden spoon sticking up out of one fist like a frozen banner. "Now, calm down," he went on. "I know ole Marcus promised to come running whenever you called for help. And I'll do my best, but, first, let me think a little."

He held the door open for her. "Come on in while I finish cleaning up after my supper," he added.

She followed him into a room that seemed to serve as

166

parlor, bedroom, and kitchen, all in one. A wooden bedstead covered with a faded patchwork quilt filled one corner, with a washstand holding a cracked pitcher and bowl beside it. A rocking chair and another wooden chair sat before a brick fireplace, where a small iron kettle hung from a crane, much like the one in their cabin back in Kentucky. Sarah caught a whiff of mustard greens and corn bread. Her stomach growled emptily.

"You hungry, missy?" Marcus asked quickly, and she felt her face flush with embarrassment that he had heard. But she was starved! It had been a long time since the noon meal.

He motioned her to one of two mismatched chairs pushed under a small table by the fireplace. She pulled out one of them and sat down, watching him ladle greens, with a small piece of fat pork on top, onto a tin plate. He sat the plate on the table in front of her, and bent over a griddle on the hearth to cut her a piece of corn bread. He laid it beside her plate.

"Sorry, I won't have any butter until my cow freshens, but there's cider vinegar there on the table," he said, placing a fork beside the plate and handing her a second dish towel to use for a napkin. "You eat a bite, while I try to think what to do."

Sarah took the fork and pushed the fat pork aside. Then she reached for the vinegar and sprinkled it over the greens. She began to eat. Marcus dipped a wooden dipper into a bucket and filled a stoneware mug with water, and she drank from it thirstily, washing down the tart greens and dry bread.

"We'll need horses and a carriage," he mused, swinging the crane away from the fire, and wrapping the leftover corn bread in a cloth to keep it fresh.

"Just horses will do, Marcus," she answered around a mouthful of greens. "I rode to Virginia from Kentucky on horseback. And a carriage will only slow us down."

He nodded. "We'll have to get permission from your folks. Your uncle knows me well, but I don't know if he will . . ."

"Oh, no, Marcus!" she cried in alarm. "They would never let me go! You mustn't ask!"

"But, Miss Sarah, I can't take you off to Norfolk without the consent of your family!"

"Marcus, please!" she begged. "They will never agree!"

"But, missy . . ."

"I know!" she interrupted his protest. "I'll leave them a note to find after we're well on our way. By the time they read it, we'll be halfway home!"

He shook his head stubbornly. "Aw, no, Miss Sarah. I could get in a heap of trouble . . ."

"All right!" she said, getting up from the table. "I thought you would help me. You're the only friend I have in Williamsburg, now that Gabrielle . . ." She abandoned that sentence, and said, "I'll just have to find some other way, then." She headed for the door.

"Now, hold on, missy!" Marcus called after her, slipping the hole in the handle of the wooden spoon over a nail in the fireplace mantel. "Ole Marcus will do his best to help." He sighed. "I'm pretty sure the governor would trust me with a couple of horses. But I just can't take you traipsing around over the countryside without Colonel Armstrong's blessing!"

She gave him a thin smile that would have done Aunt Charity credit. "It's all right, Marcus. I'm sorry to have bothered you, and I'm much obliged for the supper." With that, she left the cottage, closing the red door firmly behind her.

She half expected him to come running after her. When he didn't, she walked dejectedly down the path and across the fields, trying to think of some way to carry out her plan to overtake Gabrielle.

She supposed she would have to borrow one of Uncle Ethan's horses, perhaps the one he had sent with Nate to carry her from Kentucky. The horse was gentle and had obeyed her well.

Sarah didn't want to go back to the Armstrong house, but she knew it would be better if she did. She could go to bed with the rest of the family, then slip out later when everyone was asleep. This would give her a head start on anyone who might come after her.

Sarah crept back inside the house just as the family was sitting down to supper. Her stomach rejected the sight of fried chicken and biscuits with rich milk gravy. She had to pretend to eat, though. She couldn't risk arousing suspicion. Still, she was full of greens and corn bread!

"What's wrong, Sarah, are you ill?" Aunt Charity asked finally. "You've hardly touched your chicken."

"And it's your favorite!" Megan said, chewing on a crispy drumstick. "Mine too!" she added.

"That's obvious!" Tabitha said, pointing to the pile of bones on her little sister's plate.

Sarah laughed with them, trying again to finish the wing she had allowed Aunt Charity to put on her plate. "I . . . I don't feel very well," she excused herself.

"It's all right, Sarah," Uncle Ethan said kindly. "You've had a very trying day, and I think your mind is occupied with something besides food."

She looked up in alarm. Had he read her mind? Had he, somehow, discovered her plans? She didn't want to deceive him again. If only she could take the horse, ride after Gabrielle, and be back before they awoke in the morning! Surely the militiamen guarding Gabrielle would make camp for the night close by. It must have been late in the afternoon when they left Williamsburg. Surely they wouldn't travel far by night!

Finally, the meal and a long evening in the parlor, spent listening to Abigail's harpsichord tinkle out her father's favorite tunes, were over, and they all went upstairs to bed.

Sarah lay in the big bed beside Abigail, waiting for sleep to overtake the household.

20

Sarah felt the icy fingers of fear brush the back of her neck as she rode down the deserted road beneath a black, empty sky. She threw a glance over her shoulder. Were those horses' hooves she heard? But the night wrapped itself around everything, as thick as a quilt stuffed with goose feathers. On either side of her, the dark forest rose up, with an occasional pair of yellow eyes watching in silence as she passed.

She dug her heels into the little mare's sides, urging her on through the mud. Sarah had been so wrapped up in her plan to see Gabrielle again that she hadn't thought about how scary it would be out alone in the middle of the night, with wild animals and redcoats and maybe even robbers lurking in the trees.

Again, she thought she heard horses' hooves behind her. She strained to hear above the plopping of the mare's feet along the muddy road. She couldn't be very far from

Williamsburg. Was Uncle Ethan already on her trail? Had he gone out to the stables and found Gracie missing? Had he caught on to her questions at supper about the route to Norfolk?

She had wasted too much time saddling and bridling the horse, she thought. Gracie, the little brown mare she had ridden from Kentucky, had recognized her and stood quietly while Sarah slipped the bridle over her head and the bit into her mouth. But it had been more difficult to fasten the saddle girth under Gracie's stomach than she had realized, and her head start before Uncle Ethan found her note was cut short.

Suddenly, a horse whinnied behind her. Gracie gave an answering whinny. "Shhh!" Sarah ordered. It could be Uncle Ethan behind her. Or, worse, it could be a redcoat soldier, or even a robber! Of course, she had nothing worth stealing, except, perhaps, the little tin cup she had tucked into her pocket for Gabrielle. A robber, though, wouldn't know that she had nothing of value.

She pulled Gracie to the side of the road, slipped off her back, and led her into the trees. Sarah prayed that her follower would not hear the faint creak of the leather saddle or the jingle of metal on the bridle.

She could see the barest outline of a horse and rider now, coming toward her at a fast pace. She held her breath as they went past and were lost in the darkness ahead.

The sound of hooves had barely died away, and she had just started back toward the road, when she heard more hooves, coming again from the direction of Williamsburg. Sarah shrank back into the trees, listening to her heart pounding against her ribs. Surely it could be heard down on the road!

Then the approaching horse whinnied. She wrapped both hands around the mare's mouth and nose to keep her from answering. Even so, Gracie gave a little ripple of sound from deep in her throat.

Horse and rider stopped dead still in the center of the road. "Easy, Jake!" the man said softly. "Ole Marcus hears something over there in the woods."

Marcus! Was it truly Marcus, or had she imagined the softly spoken name? And if it were Marcus, had he changed his mind and decided to help her after all? Or had he been sent by Uncle Ethan to bring her home? There was no way to find answers to her questions without revealing her presence.

"Miss Sarah?" he called softly. "Is that you there in the woods?"

All at once, Sarah no longer cared why he had come. She was just glad he was there. She led Gracie toward the road, calling, "Marcus! It's me! Sarah! I'm here!"

He dismounted and came toward her. He bent and held his hands for her to place her foot on like a mounting block, and swung her up onto the mare's back. He then walked over to the horse he was riding.

"Colonel Armstrong let me borrow Jake to come after you," he explained.

"First, Gabrielle, and then you, Marcus," she said angrily. "Why did you betray me to Uncle Ethan? He probably wouldn't have found my note until morning!" She felt more bold now that she was no longer alone.

"Well, missy," he answered, swinging back up into Jake's saddle in one easy motion, "I got to thinking how dangerous it is out here on the road at night, especially for a young lady traveling alone, and I just couldn't let you do it. And, as I told you, I couldn't come with you without your family's permission. Besides, I have no horse of my own." He chuckled, then said seriously, "But, as I was talking with your uncle, a messenger came from the governor, telling the colonel that Devon has escaped from gaol."

Sarah gasped, remembering the lone rider who had galloped past her just minutes ago. Could it have been Alistair? She shivered at the thought of encountering the cold-eyed, coldhearted spy out there alone in the darkness. Then she related to Marcus what she had seen and heard.

"If it was the wily Devon, he will likely make his way through the woods to the James River, where his boatman is probably still lurking, just in case he shows up," Marcus said. He sighed. "At any rate, he won't get far. Colonel Armstrong himself is heading up the search party. That's why he couldn't come after you, and sent me."

"And I suppose Uncle Ethan gave you strict orders to bring me straight home!" she muttered, still angry in spite of her relief at having company out there in the darkness.

"Well, now, Miss Sarah, Colonel Armstrong said I was to bring you home, but I don't recall him saying exactly how to do it."

"What do you mean, Marcus?" Sarah asked impatiently, tired of his games.

"I figure," he went on, "so long as we get home about dawn, it won't matter how we go about it, or if we take a little detour."

"Detour?"

"Aye, missy, I figure we could rest here awhile, then

turn around and head back to Williamsburg. Or, in about the same amount of time, we could ride as hard as we can toward Norfolk, overtake a certain party, and still get back to Williamsburg at about sunup."

"Oh, Marcus!" she cried. "Thank you! I . . . I don't know how to thank you!"

"Nonsense," he said. "I'm sure your uncle would want us to warn the militia of Devon's escape. He could try some scheme to help his lady spy escape with him! Now, just let Gracie drop in behind Jake here, and if they're taking the lady to Norfolk by carriage—and I'm sure they are—we will overtake them long before dawn, for we have no carriage to coax through the mud."

So for the next couple of hours Sarah dozed in the saddle as Gracie obediently followed Jake's steadily moving form down the road. It was still very dark when she was awakened by the mare coming to a complete stop.

"Why are we stop? . . ." she began sleepily.

"Shhh!" Marcus warned.

Then she heard it too—the creaking of leather and the groaning of wooden carriage wheels ahead of them. She turned to look questioningly at Marcus, but she couldn't see his face in the darkness.

Suddenly they were surrounded by men on horseback. Sarah stifled a scream as a gruff voice called, "Who goes there?"

"It's Marcus, from the Governor's Palace!" he answered quickly. "And Colonel Ethan Armstrong's niece. We bring you warning from the colonel!"

A militiaman rode closer, holding a lantern up to light their faces. Sarah gasped as she saw guns aimed at them from all sides. Then she recognized the lantern holder. It

was Seth Coler! Tabitha would be glad to know where he was, but she would be upset to find out that he really was involved in the war.

"My cousin, Tabitha, sends you her best wishes," she whispered impulsively. In the lantern's glow, she saw a puzzled frown crease his forehead under his tricornered hat. "The girl who comes to watch you slop the pigs at Chowning's," she explained. Then a pleased grin chased the frown away. He cleared his throat and stared ahead of him, trying to look military and important, Sarah guessed. She could still see the hint of a smile, however.

Marcus pulled a paper out of his shirt and held it out to the men, but the one who appeared to be the leader shook his head. "Save it for the captain!" he snapped. "Men, surround them and take them to the carriage. Captain Randolph will want to question them."

★ Chapter Twenty ★

Just around the bend, Sarah saw the black shape of a carriage stopped beside the road, its lanterns flickering against the darkness.

The captain held Marcus's paper up under the side light of the carriage. Then he peered closely into Marcus's face. "Why, it is Marcus!" he exclaimed. "What are you doing out here on the road on such a night? Man, don't you know this free paper won't protect you if you fall into the wrong hands? Why, this paper could be destroyed, and gold would end up in somebody's pocket from the sale of a new slave to some southern cotton plantation!"

He handed the paper back to Marcus, and turned to Sarah. "And who might you be?" he asked.

"I . . . I'm Colonel Ethan Armstrong's niece, sir, Sarah Moore, from Kentucky," she stammered, trying not to look at the carriage. She suspected Gabrielle sat in there listening to all they said, just as she had sat in Christiana Campbell's and the Raleigh Tavern picking up war secrets to pass on to her fellow spy.

"Colonel Armstrong was preparing to escort Miss Sarah on a small journey when Governor Henry sent for him to head up the search party for Devon," Marcus explained. "Pelham has let the spy escape!"

Sarah heard a gasp from deep inside the carriage.

"No!" the Captain breathed. "You mean there was no guard posted at the gaol except Pelham? With the most infamous British spy in history lodged there? This will warrant looking into, my man, and Pelham had better have his excuses lined up like ducks in a row!"

He rode around the carriage, giving orders to his men, checking the chains that secured the door handles of the vehicle.

"Where are you headed, Marcus?" he asked when he came back.

"Norfolk, sir," Marcus answered truthfully. "But, Captain, Colonel Armstrong's niece is exhausted, about to fall from her saddle. Is there anything? . . ."

"Let her ride in the carriage," the captain interrupted. "Our lady spy won't harm her. The young lady can rest awhile."

The next thing Sarah knew, she was seated inside the carriage next to Gabrielle.

21

Chérie, you have come!" Gabrielle exclaimed softly. She leaned forward, the glow from the carriage's lanterns reflected in her dark eyes. She took both of Sarah's hands in hers.

"Yes, Mademoiselle," Sarah answered. But, now that she had found Gabrielle, she had lost all the words she had planned to say.

She pulled one hand free, reached into her pocket, and took out the little tin cup. "I want you to have this," she managed to say, placing the cup in Gabrielle's hand. "I bought it the day I met you, back before anything happened between us, good or bad."

"I am so sorry, *chérie,* for the things I did to you. You were right. I did betray your friendship. I used one dear friend to help another. And I destroyed something very precious in the process." She stopped, unable to go on. Instead, she squeezed Sarah's hand.

Sarah didn't know how to answer. She sat silently until the driver flicked his whip, and the carriage lurched forward.

"Did you know that Alistair has escaped from gaol?" she said finally.

"*Oui.* And don't misunderstand me, Sarah. I do not regret for a moment helping Alistair, only that I used you to do it. I would do the same things again, but I would do them differently. *Ah, chérie,* I would give my life for the opportunity to do them differently!"

Again, Sarah did not know what to say.

"You are such a bright pupil, so eager to learn, and so exciting to teach! I had grown so fond of you, and now I have spoiled it all. You can never forgive me, and I don't blame you, *chérie.*" She pulled her hand away to cover her face. "I do not deserve your forgiveness," she cried.

Sarah reached out to comfort her, and felt the wetness of real tears on her face. "But I have forgiven you, Mademoiselle," she said. Then, all the things she had thought while standing in front of the milliner's shop came tumbling out.

"You have given me so much, Gabrielle," she finished. "You have opened my thoughts to so many wonderful things, things that will go with me for the rest of my life! And when the bad thoughts come, I will replace them with those, and think of you with gratitude and . . ." she stumbled over the word, then finished, ". . . with love."

Gabrielle gave Sarah a quick embrace. "I will always remember you, *chérie,* as the sunlight that touched briefly a very dark and lonely time of my life. And I will cherish this cup for as long as I shall live."

"The etching on the cup represents the American

colonies becoming a free nation, and you may not like that," Sarah said. "But maybe it can remind you simply of one wild Kentuckian and the freedom she holds dear."

"As I once told you, *m'amie*, my French and English blood wars in my veins. Had it not been for Alistair, I might have felt differently about this American Revolution." She was silent a moment, then added, "When this war is over, and it will not endanger you for me to do so, I shall write you and tell you where I am. Perhaps you will find it in your heart to answer my letter."

"I would like that, Gabrielle," Sarah whispered, as the carriage jerked to a halt and the door opened.

"Another storm is brewing, Miss Sarah," Marcus said loudly, "and I have told the captain that I am sure Colonel Armstrong would want us to return home and resume our journey on a better day."

She knew he was making a way for them to get back to Williamsburg before dawn. He had given her this moment with Gabrielle. She could not ask for more.

"I believe you are right, Marcus," she agreed, loudly enough for the captain, riding beside the carriage, to hear. She turned to embrace Gabrielle one last time.

Then she was out of the carriage, on the mare's back, and riding toward Williamsburg behind Jake and Marcus, through the rising wind, as fast as the mud would allow.

They were moving too fast for conversation, so Sarah gave herself over to replaying in her thoughts all that had passed between her and Gabrielle in the carriage. She was so glad she had seen her and been able to tell her she had forgiven her. It would have been awful knowing they had parted enemies, after all the hours of companionship they had shared in the little brown house.

Pictures flashed through her mind of Gabrielle teaching her and her cousins to serve tea, to curtsy, to embroider; of the two of them bent over her evening studies, Gabrielle correcting, encouraging, praising. She sighed. Would she ever have another tutor who could open for her the windows of the world as Gabrielle had done? Surely she would not find one with Gabrielle's wit and charm. But Sarah also knew that she would not be fooled again by someone like Gabrielle. She felt very old and wise, and, suddenly, very tired.

She supposed she would be in a great amount of trouble when she got back to Williamsburg. How could she ever make up for all the worry she had caused? She had been so bent on doing things her way!

"I'd give my life for the opportunity to do things differently," Gabrielle had said. Sarah knew how she felt.

She wished there were some way she could move time backward to the happy days before she had taken her uncle's papers, before she had gone off on her own to find Gabrielle. She knew she deserved any punishment her aunt and uncle might give her. She had been unforgivably foolish and headstrong.

"You must forgive to be forgiven," Marcus had told her. Well, she had forgiven Gabrielle. If she asked Uncle Ethan and Aunt Charity to forgive her this one last time, would they? Would God? Marcus said God was always ready to forgive if someone were truly sorry.

Sarah saw ahead of her that Marcus had stopped his horse at the corner of Nicholson Street. Then she realized that she could see him, sitting on Jake's back, waiting for her to catch up with him. The sky was beginning to lighten.

"Miss Sarah, I hope you know how much danger you were in tonight, out there on that road alone," he began when she reached him.

"Marcus," she broke in, "I promise I will never do such a stupid thing again! I was so scared until you found me! But I had to see her! And it was worth any sacrifice," she added.

He studied her for a moment. "The Good Book says, 'To obey is better than sacrifice,' " he said solemnly. Then he nodded his head, as though satisfied with the quick guilt and regret reflected in her eyes before she dropped her gaze from his. He turned Jake and rode on down Nicholson Street.

Though the sun's rays were beginning to spill over the trees at the eastern end of the street, the Armstrong house was still in shadow as they tied their horses to the hitching post and went up the walk.

Uncle Ethan was waiting in the hallway when Sarah opened the door.

"Thank you, Marcus," he said. "Would you please put the mare in the stables? You may ride Jake home and return him later."

"Thank you, sir. I'm much obliged to you, Colonel Armstrong," Marcus answered, "but Jake's tired, too, and ole Marcus has no proper place for him to rest. I'll just see to it that both horses are rubbed down and tended to, and then I'll go on home. Good night, Miss Sarah," he added, turning to leave.

"Thank you, Marcus," she said fervently. "Thank you so much!"

"You may go to bed, Sarah," her uncle said, as he shut the door. "I have read your note, and we will discuss this later, after we've both had some rest. I am exhausted, as I suspect you are."

He walked to the stairs, then turned to face her in the growing light. "My mission was successful," he said seriously, "was yours?"

"Yes, sir," she answered, returning his look steadily.

He put one hand on her shoulder. "I'm glad, Sarah," he said, "I really am. But will you promise me one thing?" It was impossible to read his expression in the dim hallway.

Sarah took a deep breath. "Yes, sir," she answered, knowing she was in no position to refuse, after all the trouble she had caused.

"Don't keep any more secrets from me, please? I'm getting too old for all this excitement!" He grinned down at her, but his weary sigh was real, she thought, as she followed him up the stairs.

Sarah went into Abigail's room, undressed, and put on

her long, white gown. She started toward the bed, then turned and padded down the hall into Megan's room. She crawled into bed beside her little cousin and pulled the thick quilt over her shoulders.

Tomorrow, she thought, yawning, she would ask forgiveness for all she had done. Uncle Ethan's attitude tonight hinted that it would be granted. If so, she vowed she would be so obedient she would never need to ask again! She would be content here, too, until she went back home, and she would do her best to get along with everybody in the Armstrong household. Even Abigail!

The wind whistled softly around the eaves of the house and whispered through the cedar outside Megan's window. Suddenly, Sarah remembered what Marcus had said about God trying to speak to them on the wind. It that were true, she wanted to hear what He had to say. She really did. But she was just too tired now to listen.

She turned over on her side and snuggled closer to Meggie. Maybe, like Uncle Ethan, God would talk to her tomorrow, she thought drowsily, feeling herself sinking into sleep.

Echoes from the Past

When Sarah came to Williamsburg in 1777, it was a thriving little town of busy shops and taverns scattered along Duke of Gloucester Street, with the Colonial Capitol at one end and the College of William and Mary at the other. Charming brick or wooden houses, with steep gabled roofs and small-paned windows, surrounded Duke of Gloucester, and behind each of them was a fenced garden filled with herbs, flowers, shrubs, and trees.

The shops on Duke of Gloucester Street sold merchandise brought down the James River. The goods came from Boston, Massachusetts, from England, France, or Italy, and included spices, buttons, and ribbons. Sarah could buy a piece of ribbon for her dress or hair for a farthing (about a penny).

Williamsburg had many craftsmen who sold their wares in the town. The blacksmith made nails, candle holders, hinges, and horseshoes. The cooper made barrels, buckets, and wooden utensils. The printer and bookbinder turned out newspapers and broadsides (large, one-page announcements), and leather-bound books. The brick maker made bricks to pave the streets and construct houses and shops. The lumberyard provided clapboards for the outside and lumber for the inside of Williamsburg buildings.

The taverns (restaurants) served hearty meals and provided sleeping rooms for travelers. Strolling musicians entertained diners with tunes played on the violin, mandolin, flute, or hornpipe. Some taverns, like the Raleigh and the Kings Arms, were gathering places for the wealthy, the educated, the political leaders of the day. Colonial men were not ashamed to have their wives and families accompany them there for a meal.

Taverns like Chowning's and Shield's catered to the less genteel (well-bred), and gaming (gambling) was common there. Sometimes the patrons drank too much "hard" cider (fermented apple juice) or other strong drinks and spent a night in the local gaol (pronounced jail) with criminals, prisoners of war, and those who could not pay their debts.

Christiana Campbell's tavern on Waller Street, down by the Capitol, was less fashionable than the Raleigh, but not so bawdy (vulgar) as Chowning's or Shield's. George Washington, Patrick Henry, Thomas Jefferson, and other Patriots sometimes met there or at the Raleigh to discuss plans, like those overheard by Gabrielle Gordon and passed on to the Demon Devon.

Some poor men and women who were seeking their fortunes, came to America as indentured servants. Like Sarah's friend Betsy, they agreed to work for a certain number of years for anyone who would pay their passage across the ocean. When their debt of passage was paid by their agreed years of work, they were free to live their own lives.

Not all colonists were poor, however. Many were wealthy in their own right. Some were well educated and wanted good schools for their sons. In 1693, long before Sarah was even born, the Virginia General Assembly sent the Reverend James Blair to England to ask King William and Queen Mary to establish a college in Williamsburg so ". . . that the youth may be piously educated," as he put it, "and the Christian Faith may be propagated amongst the Western Indians, to the Glory of Almighty God." To this day, the College of William and Mary is busy educating students.

Girls were not allowed to go to school in Sarah's time. They were either taught at home by their mothers, grandmother, or aunts, or they had tutors. Even with a tutor, most colonial girls did not study Latin or history or geography, as Sarah did with Gabrielle Gordon. They learned to sew and embroider, to manage a household, to play the piano or harpsichord, to write or accept invitations, to be a gracious hostess, to curtsy, and to dance.

Worship was important to most of the citizens of Williamsburg. But even if it hadn't been, all white Virginians were required by law to attend church at least once each month. The official religion was the Church of England (Episcopal), and Bruton Parish Church was the official church of Williamsburg. Services were held every Sunday morning and on Christmas Day and Good Friday. These services included readings from the Book of Common Prayer and a sermon. Holy Communion was served four times a year.

★ Stranger in Williamsburg ★

African Americans in Williamsburg—free or slave—attended Bruton Parish Church also, but they sat in the gallery upstairs instead of on the red velvet cushions inside the high-walled pews, where Sarah and her cousins sat. At the time Sarah came to stay with her Aunt Charity's family, there were an equal number of African Americans and whites living in Williamsburg. Most of the African Americans were slaves, but some, like Marcus, were free.

Williamsburg was a pleasant, peaceful place to live and carry on business—until the British government began to demand more and more taxes from the colonists. The colonists were not allowed to send representatives to Parliament to participate in making the laws under which they had to live, which they quickly began to resent.

The anger and resentment of the colonists started to show itself in the streets and taverns of Williamsburg as they discussed the latest indignities imposed on them by King George and Parliament. Colonial leaders were sent to talk with King George, but they found that, as Sarah's brother Nate said, King George "danced to Parliament's tune like a puppet on a string." And Parliament was only interested in adding money to its treasury; they couldn't have cared less about what the colonists thought.

Finally, Patrick Henry's soul-stirring words rang out: "I know not what course others may take, but as for me, give me liberty or give me death!" Soon afterward, the Patriots of Virginia told the world they would be free of English rule, and the rest of the colonies agreed. The war for independence had begun.

The King's Governor and his family fled to England for safety, along with other Tories (people who were loyal to the King of England). And Patrick Henry, the new Commonwealth (state) of Virginia's first governor, moved into the Governor's Palace.

The young colonies-turned-states did not have the chance of a snowball in July of winning a war against the best-trained and best-equipped army in the world. As the red-coated British soldiers marched toward them in perfect formation, the colonists soon learned to hide behind trees, rocks, and fences, and make every bullet count. Hungry, cold, and poorly equipped, many of them died on the battlefield with Patrick Henry's words ringing in their hearts. But they prayed hard and often, and, in the end, the Patriots won. The United States of America was born.

Today you can visit restored Colonial Williamsburg and walk Duke of Gloucester Street as Sarah did. You can shop at John Greenhow's store, and stand in front of the little house on Waller Street where she studied with the milliner Gabrielle Gordon. Sample the delicious offerings of the bakery and the taverns. Stroll in the gardens of the Governor's Palace. Sit on the bank of the canal, and watch the swans.

Then get ready for another adventure with Sarah, this time back in Kentucky at the fort at Harrodstown. *Reunion in Kentucky* is on sale at your favorite Christian bookstore now.

❖ PARENTS ❖

Are you looking for fun ways to bring the Bible to life in the lives of your children?

Chariot Family Publishing has hundreds of books, toys, games, and videos that help teach your children the Bible and apply it to their everyday lives.

Look for these educational, inspirational, and fun products at your local Christian bookstore.